KIDNAPPED
SHIELA STEWART

KIDNAPPED
Published by Linden Bay Romance, 2007
Linden Bay Romance, LLC, U.S.

ISBN Trade paperback:
978-1-60202-031-3
ISBN MS Reader (LIT):
978-1-60202-030-6
Other available formats (no ISBNs are assigned):
PDF, PRC & HTML
Copyright © SHIELA STEWART, 2007
ALL RIGHTS RESERVED

The work is protected by copyright and should not be copied without permission. Linden Bay Romance, LLC reserves all rights. Re-use or re-distribution of any and all materials is prohibited under law.

This is a work of fiction and any resemblance to persons, living or dead, or business establishments, events or locales is coincidental.

Cover art by Dan Skinner

To my soul mate, William. Without your love, support, and belief in me, I would not be who I am today.

Chapter 1

Her head throbbed with the mother of all headaches. And who wouldn't have a headache after listening to the incessant nattering of the two most boring people in the world? Liz pushed through the restaurant doors and into the hot mid morning sun, looking forward to spending a good three hours at the spa, relaxing.

She simply didn't know why she continued these weekly brunches with Bonnie and Moira; the two irritated the hell out of her. Actually, she did—it was for her father, who insisted Liz align herself with the 'right' sort of people. What on earth could possibly be right where Bonnie and Moira were concerned, aside from the fact that they came from money and everyone knew them? They were the epitome of snobby rich and so not like her.

She pulled the keys from her purse and noticed her hand bag looked a little worn. Maybe after her spa treatment she should go shopping for a new bag. She was entitled, after all, having to deal with the gossipy twosome for the last few hours.

Flipping her long hair over her shoulder, Liz hurried to her car, her Prada heels clicking as she walked. Pressing the button on the remote, she engaged the engine which would automatically start up the air-conditioning. There was nothing worse than getting into a hot car.

She was going to enjoy being pampered.

Approaching her car, she frowned, seeing the dark, dusty, blue van parked unforgivably close to it. Squeezing through the minimal opening, careful not to soil her slacks on the dirty van, Liz reached for the car door. She heard the van doors behind her slide open. A hand clamped over her mouth and another grabbed her around the waist. In the time it took her to think to scream, she was yanked into the van and the doors slammed shut.

Before she had a chance to utter a single word in protest, someone shoved a cloth in her mouth and tied it tightly around her head. For a split second she saw the hands as they lifted a cloth to her eyes, covering up her sight. As the shock began to wear off, Liz came to the alarming revelation.

She was being kidnapped.

Despite the rag in her mouth, she screamed, though it came out muffled. Using her best defense, she began to kick wildly with her legs, her fists stabbing at air. There was no damn way she was going to sit still and let this happen to *her*.

Her foot connected with something solid and when she heard the wild cursing, she knew she'd hit her abductor. So she kept kicking and flailing with her hands.

"God damn bitch."

The force of the blow to her jaw knocked her back, hitting her head on the floor as she fell. Stars exploded before her covered eyes as the pain ricocheted from her jaw to her head. The nausea began to build in her gut and she thought she might vomit as he rolled her onto her stomach, then held her.

She yelped when he yanked her arms back and tied them roughly together by the wrists.

"Serves you right."

His nails scraped her bare feet as he ripped the shoes from her feet. What the hell was going to happen to her? What did he have planned to do with her? She began to panic, her breathing rapid as she rolled herself over. Pulling her legs to her chest, she prayed for someone to save her.

It startled her when the van began to roll and she realized there was more than one abductor. She felt every bump as the vehicle bounced on the road, making her already jittery stomach swirl like a tornado. She swallowed it back, demanding her body not expel the contents of her breakfast because she knew the outcome would not be a pleasant one. Not with the gag over her mouth. It seemed that they drove forever, stopping here and there for moments, then rolling along again.

She knew he was near because she could hear his breathing. Her mind foggy, she couldn't think above the pain. What should she do? What should she do?

When the van stopped and she heard a door open, then close, she sucked in a deep breath, her stomach tense as she prepared for the worse. The screech of metal startled her as the sliding door opened. Her heart began to race so fast she thought she might pass out.

"Grab her legs."

"Her mouth is bleeding."

"Yeah." He laughed.

She felt hands sliding under her back as another set grabbed hold of her ankles. Her body tensed as they lifted and shifted her. Where were they taking her?

"Let me go," she mumbled through the cloth in her mouth, jerking her body in an attempt to break free.

"Hold her."

"I've got her."

His hands slid under her arm pits and grabbed hold of her breasts. She felt the nausea rising up in her throat.

"Cut it out."

"Oh come on, I'm just having a little fun."

"There's no need for that."

Liz heard a door creak, keys jingling, then another door opening. There wasn't another sound to be heard anywhere. Silence still in the air, Liz wondered where she'd been taken.

"I can take her from here."

"I've already got a good grip."

One voice was deep, the other whiny and higher in tone. The one with the higher tone had been in the back of the van with her, and the one who'd hit her. How many others were there?

The way they shifted her, she judged that she was being carried up a flight of stairs, and from the sound of the stairs, they weren't carpeted. The one holding her feet wore boots of some sort that made a clomping sound as he stepped. And the one near her head wore softer soled shoes, maybe running shoes. His hands were soft, despite the brutality, and he wore something with buttons down the front. He smelt like cheap cologne and sweat. Everything she could, she put to memory. Even if she couldn't see her abductors, at least she could identify them by smell and sound.

"Set her down on the chair."

The deep voiced one. She felt the chair beneath her butt, then hands pressing her down. The instant the hands slid from around her chest, she bolted up, attempting to break free. It didn't matter that she couldn't see, she wasn't going to sit still while they did God knew what to her.

"Hold her down, damn it."

"I didn't think she would make a break for it."

The hand that grabbed her viciously yanked her down, planting her hard into the chair, and when he leaned down and whispered in her ear, she knew it was the snooty one.

"Try that again and I'll knock you so hard you won't remember your name."

"Hey, settle down."

"Just tie her up already."

The one with the deep voice didn't seem to care much for the snooty voiced one. She felt something brush over her chest and she tensed up. When it pulled against her, she realized they were tying her up with a rope. "Please, let me go," she mumbled through the cloth.

"Not going to happen, sweetheart."

The deep voiced one was tying her up. He had a different smell to him, something familiar. Calvin, he wore Calvin cologne and he wore boots of some sort, his voice was deep and he didn't seem to like his partner. *Remember it, Liz, remember every detail.*

"There, that should hold her."

She flinched as the hands touched the back of her

head, then realized they were untying her blind fold. It slid away and she blinked rapidly, trying to get her eyes to focus. The hands worked at the back of her head once more, untying the gag.

"Please, please just let me go." She wished she could rub her eyes to make them focus.

"Maybe you should have left the gag over her mouth."

Her eyes shifted to her left where the voice came from. Through her blurred vision, she could make out the figure standing at her side. Blinking her lashes, she saw he wore a mask, a female mask, and he was tall and thin. He wore a silk green shirt with buttons running along the front. And as her eyes focused she looked into the mask of Betty Rubble.

"She's secured, we can go now."

Her head turned to her right and to the big man moving out from behind her. He wore a white polo style shirt, blue jeans and work boots, and as he turned to face her, she saw the Bart Simpson mask that covered his entire head, save the eyes and mouth.

She'd been abducted by Betty Rubble and Bart Simpson.

"What are you planning to do with me?"

Betty Rubble turned to her and when he laughed her body tensed up. It reminded her of a creepy murderer's laugh she'd heard so many times in the movies.

"Everything I possibly can."

Her heart thundered with fear and as she watched them leaving the room, she wished she could wake up from this horrible nightmare.

~

"What the hell is wrong with you?"

"I'm just having some fun."

"Well, lay off it already. This isn't real, Terry, remember that." Pulling the mask from his face, tossing it on the table as he passed it by, Mac ran a hand through his dark hair in frustration. Pushing through the screen door he stepped out into the hot sun and looked out at the property before him.

He couldn't understand why the banks wouldn't give him an extension on his mortgage and he again wished there'd been some other way to get the money to save his property rather than abducting a woman. He'd had no choice, he reminded himself as he slid behind the wheel of the van. He had a month to come up with the money to save his father's farm, his home, and this just fell into his lap at the right time.

He started the van and pulled it around back to the garage. And besides, she was safe with him. It wasn't real, like he'd told Terry.

Then why did he have this sickening feeling in the pit of his belly?

Chapter 2

The tears rolled down her cheeks as they fell from her eyes. She didn't wail like some women did, but instead she cried silently. She'd always been a silent crier. Why was this happening to her? What had she done to deserve this? She was a good person; she never hurt anyone, so why was she being punished? The tears fell in silence, dropping onto her lap to dampen her tan slacks.

What were they going to do to her? Oh God, they could do all manner of things to her. Did anyone even notice her missing? What would her parents do when they found out? What if she didn't make it out of this alive? Oh God, she didn't want to die. She remembered Betty Rubble's response to her question and the sickness rolled in her belly. His hands had been on her breasts, squeezing them as he carried her from the van. If he intended to kill her, it wouldn't be before he had some fun with her. She needed to think; she needed to get out of here and fast.

Shaking off the tears, stiffening her chin, Liz took a moment to look around. They'd put her in a bedroom—why would they tie you up in a bedroom if they didn't intend on having their way with you? Their intentions clear, Liz scrambled to think. She needed to get free from the ropes that held her body in place, so she began to wiggle, trying to loosen them. They stung her hands, and she bit back the pain, knowing she would experience worse if she simply sat here doing nothing.

She was on the upper floor; she continued to think as she shifted trying to break free. And from the sounds of the silence, they weren't in the city any longer. Where had they taken her? It didn't matter, she told herself, shifting her shoulders, feeling the ropes slide over her arm. The instant she could manage to free herself of the ropes she would make a run for it.

Where were they? They'd left her alone in the room, but she doubted very much they had left altogether. That meant they were in the house somewhere. But where? It didn't matter; she could climb from the window. She'd done it before, sneaking from her room at night to go out and party, or that time she'd been pursued by the paparazzi while dining with a friend. They'd hounded her all through the meal, insisting she give them an exclusive of the married man she'd been seeing. Excusing herself from the table, she'd gone to the washroom. The windows had been small, but she managed to slide herself through and make a break for it, leaving the paparazzi waiting for her.

She'd had plenty of run-ins with the tabloids and the leeches they sent out to capture any unsavory thing she might be involved with. And when they couldn't find anything, they'd made it up. She'd lived a lifetime of being in the spot light, thanks to her famous father, Jonathan Cromwell. Though lately there hadn't been as many roles as he would have liked. In his day, he'd been renowned for his stage performances and his big screen adaptations of villains and criminals.

And now, his only daughter had been abducted. She needed to get her butt in gear, stop whining and feeling sorry for herself, and get a grip on the situation.

She struggled once more with the ropes, frustrated that they weren't coming undone fast enough. When she heard the foot steps clomping on the stairs, her heart began to race and her mind panicked. She heard the jingle of what sounded like keys, then the door knob turned and the door began to open.

Oh God, oh God, oh God.

As he stepped through the door, she looked up into the face of Bart. Her earlier assessment of him was grossly understated. He wasn't just big, he was tall and muscular. The other guy had been the brutal one, but this guy looked scary.

"How you doing there?"

"Why are you doing this to me?" Her voice sounded far too weak and she berated herself for it. Hold your chin up, Liz, be strong.

He slipped a cigarette package from his shirt pocket and pulled one out. "Why do you think?"

She watched him put the cigarette between his lips and thought how ridiculous he looked smoking with that child's mask on. "Money? You want money, fine, I have lots of money, just name your price." She would easily give up everything she possessed if he let her go.

"It's already in the works, princess; don't worry that pretty head of yours."

"Princess? I'm not a princess? You have me mistaken with someone else." They'd abducted the wrong person; they'd mistaken her for royalty. Thank God, now that he knew his mistake, he could let her go.

"Elizabeth Cromwell, twenty eight, only daughter of Jonathan and Liza Cromwell. I know who you are, and the woman I see before me definitely looks like a princess."

Damn it, there hadn't been a mistake. Now what? "Fine, you know who I am, then you know I can get you all the money you need, but you have to let me go first."

He stared at her while he smoked for a few minutes, then shook his head. The deep rumble of his laughter startled her. "Sweetheart, you don't have money, your daddy does, and you might as well make yourself comfortable because you aren't going anywhere anytime soon." His hand made quick tapping motions as he put the cigarette out in the ashtray on the dresser.

"Fine, my father has money, then call him, demand whatever you like and he'll pay you." Her father wouldn't hesitate to pay them to release her.

"Like I said, princess, it's already in the works. Now, you be a good girl and behave while I'm gone."

She watched as he turned to leave, tripping over an untied bootlace. Stumbling forward, he managed to right himself quickly enough. He stiffened his back, yanking the door open then shutting it behind him with a solid click. The giggle escaped from her lips and startled her. For a brief moment she saw a glimmer of sunshine in her very cloudy situation.

~

Bending down, Mac tied the loose lace, making sure to tie it tight this time. *Some abductor you are*, he thought to himself, *tripping over your boot laces*. Lifting back up, he pulled the mask from his face, messing up his curly black hair. He took the stairs down directly to the kitchen. Setting his mask on the counter, he helped himself to a cup of coffee. It was, after all, his home.

"What are you doing?" he asked Terry, who was sitting at the table, writing in some sort of book.

"Writing down my experiences. I think this will look good on my resumé."

"Are you insane? You can't put that you took part in an abduction. What the hell is wrong with you, man?"

"I'm not making it factual. I'm referencing it to a movie role. They don't have to know it's not true. This is good experience for me and might come in handy."

Shaking his head, Mac added a spoon of sugar to his coffee. "I should have insisted I do this alone."

"You couldn't manage it alone Mac, and we both know it. Besides, at least you'll have company until the week is over."

Some company he wouldn't mind, but not this guy. He knew Terry Orsini as an acquaintance, but they certainly weren't friends, and not everything he knew about Terry pleased him. The guy was a pretty boy who used his looks to get what he wanted, and what he wanted most was a lucrative movie roll that would skyrocket him to the top. The other things Terry wanted were women, and he had plenty of them. But he was right in saying that Mac needed him. Two heads were better than one.

"Fine, but just remember, I deal with her, not you. Got it?"

"Yeah, sure, whatever."

His coffee in hand, he left Terry to his work and

walked into the living room, the photos on the wall catching his attention. The picture of his father with his grandchildren surrounding him on the sofa made him smile. There hadn't even been an inkling of how badly he was ailing. He'd done a good job of keeping his illness a secret, and his impending bankruptcy as well.

Now it was up to him to make sure that never happened.

For one week he could manage to keep a woman locked in his room. It would be worth it in the end when the farm he loved so dearly would be his, free and clear, and the horse ranch that he dreamt of would come to fruition.

Relaxing on the sofa, he clicked the TV on and tried to keep his mind from thinking about what he'd done.

He was, after all, responsible for kidnapping an innocent woman.

Chapter 3

Her stomach growled reminding her she hadn't eaten anything since the poached egg and croissant for brunch. She had no idea of the time, but she guessed it to be late afternoon, maybe even close to the evening. She'd been working on loosening the ropes for hours now and her wrists felt pretty raw. Clueless to where her abductors were, Liz knew that at any moment, one of them could come up to check on her. So she needed to work fast.

She wasn't going to wait around for them to get what they wanted from her father. She could hear birds chirping from somewhere behind her. Twisting her head, she tried to get a look at the window. Unable to see it clearly, she huffed.

The place didn't look new but lived in. The walls were a light creamy color but looked as if they'd been painted that way a good long time ago. From her viewpoint she could see the door off to her left and a dresser off to her right. On top sat a TV no bigger than a microwave. How did a person watch something that small?

Wiggling, she tried to get the ropes to loosen. The heat made her sweat, her face and body growing damp from the exertion. The room was hotter than a sauna. Blowing air over her face, she longed for the cool, air-conditioned apartment she lived in. Her car, she suddenly remembered, still sat in the parking lot of the restaurant. Bonnie and Moira would see it still there, and wonder what it was doing there and why it was running. Surely they would have called the police by now. Maybe someone saw her being abducted and called the police?

She wouldn't have to be rescued if it wasn't for her father's notoriety. She tugged the ropes in frustration. It had always been his fame, and she'd always been the victim of it. As far back as she could remember she had been hounded because of her father. As an infant, her parents paraded her for all to see, always dressed in the finest garments, her hair meticulously styled. She'd been sent to the finest boarding schools and spent more time there than at her home, her parents rarely having time for her. And as she matured, they insisted that she act like a lady and never do anything to sully that image, never to misbehave in public and always smile. God, there had been times she'd wanted to scream at the cameras that flashed at her from everywhere just to leave her be.

But they hadn't, and as she had grown into a young woman, they had often caught her in the arms of her companions, writing nasty stuff about her being a lush. She had been photographed leaving a party, after having a tad bit too much to drink, and stumbling as she tried to walk to her friend's car. She'd been labeled trouble from that day on, and so she had gone with it.

For years she listened to her father condemn her for not trying harder to be like him, for not accepting the roles he shifted to her, for wanting her to be someone she wasn't. So she'd rebelled, and hard. Though she hadn't touched drugs, she made good use of any bottle of alcohol handed to her. By the time she turned nineteen, she had developed a sour reputation and learned that no amount of alcohol could mask the pain she felt inside.

Under the guise of Stephanie Parsons, she fled to Paris, and to her utter relief, she hadn't been followed. She'd drawn her hair up under a plain black wig of short hair, worn dark glasses and frumpy clothing. She hadn't looked anything like herself, and it made her feel free for the first time in her life.

Until Jacques.

He entered her life, sweeping her off her feet and showed her the attention she so craved. There hadn't been any clues to lead her to believe he was married. In the five months they were together, she never suspected him of having a wife or two young children. She might never have known if she hadn't been window shopping and seen the tabloid, with her and Jacques in a heated embrace. The caption had read, 'Mistress breaks up happy family'. She bought the paper, read the story and had been devastated.

Catching the very next fight, she left Paris with the paparazzi hot on her trail, and they hadn't let up for months after the incident. Her father had been furious. Fed up with her antics, humiliating him in the public eye, he'd locked her in her room for two days. If it hadn't been for their cook, Millie, she might have gone a little insane. Not only had Millie snuck her food, but came to her at night to talk. The woman had been Liz's confidant and she'd been the one who'd told Liz she needed to make some choices in her life, choices that would allow the true Liz to come out.

But who the real Liz was, not even she knew. So she'd tried different things. The fundraisers her father insisted she do didn't interest her; school didn't look appealing, so she'd struck college from her list. She had no talent whatsoever to fall back on, though she'd been told by her acting coach that he saw potential. But she didn't want to act; it was the last thing she wanted.

Then, visiting a sick friend in the hospital, she'd stumbled onto the wrong floor. The sweetest little girl she'd ever seen approached her, asking her shyly to help her find her room. Her face had been pale against a dark head of brown thinning hair. Her brown eyes were hollow with dark circles beneath the lashes and as she lifted her arm to rub her nose, Liz saw how thin she truly was. Taking the child's hand, she led her to the nurse's station for assistance in finding her room. It was then she learned the child had terminal cancer.

When she helped her to her room, Liz saw the many faces of the children, sick with one disease or another, looking lost and lonely. She'd realized then what she wanted to do. She wanted to help the children. So she began volunteering at the hospital, reading to them or watching movies together. Once a week, she brought people in, and gave all the girls a make over. They loved those days the most. And while the girls received pampering, Liz played video games with the boys and was getting pretty damn good at it.

Today was her day off from volunteering, and she wished desperately that she hadn't listened to her father and gone out for brunch with Bonnie and Moira. She wouldn't be sitting here, tied to a rock hard chair, being held by two men with God knew what on their minds to do with her

Sighing, she worked on the ropes once more, wondering what the children would do without her if she didn't break free soon.

She heard the sound of boots on the stairs and once again her body tensed. When the door opened, she didn't know what to expect.

"Chow time, princess."

Her teeth gnashed together at the way he called her that silly nickname. Then she saw the plate in his hand and all thoughts vanished to her hunger. "You're feeding me?"

"Well it's not the finest cuisine, which I am sure you are used to, but it'll serve its purpose." Setting the plate on the nightstand, he moved in behind her and loosened the ropes on her hands. "There you go."

She pulled her hands to the front of her, gave her wrists a rub and noticed the dark red rings forming on her skin.

"Bon appetit."

She took the plate he offered and saw the plain sandwich. Lifting the top piece of bread, she saw there hadn't been much effort in constructing this sandwich. One piece of ham, processed no less, and a glop of mustard. How appetizing.

"You're welcome," he said snidely as he pulled up another chair from the corner of the room by the window.

Her lip curled as she swallowed the bland sandwich. "Thank you," she replied without a hint of the disdain she felt towards him.

Grabbing the TV remote on the bedside table, he clicked the TV on and began strolling through the channels. "How's the sandwich?"

"Fine." *Dry, lacking in taste, and whole wheat bread would have been better*, she thought snidely. "Have you contacted my father yet?" Nibbling on her sandwich, Liz examined the man before her. His chest was broad, the shirt he wore stretching to accommodate the muscles. His hair curled in black strands over the bottom of the mask. He had wide arms and big hands, long legs and big feet clad in dirty work boots. From the looks of him, he wasn't the sort you tussled with if you wanted to win.

"You don't need to concern yourself with such trivial matters, princess."

"Stop calling me that," she blurted out and instantly her eyes lifted with worry.

"I think it's suited to you." He pulled out a cigarette and casually lit it up while Liz picked her sandwich apart.

"Why, because I have money?" Good God, she'd lost her mind. He looked big enough to crush her with his bare hands and she boldly argued with him.

"There's that, plus the high and mighty attitude you exude."

She bit her tongue, preventing the many retorts that came to mind. The last thing she needed to do is piss off her abductor. "May I have something to drink?"

Without a word, he walked to the bathroom, dropped his cigarette in the toilet then taking a paper cup from the container on the wall he filled it with water. "Here you go."

Her eyes shifted to the paper cup and the water inside of it, and she cringed. "Thank you." Taking it, she sipped the tepid water, despising him even more.

"Finished eating?"

"Yes, I am." Ready to use the plate to smash him in the face, she huffed when he scooped it from her lap and placed it on the floor before she could act. If she couldn't use the plate, there were other means of defense. Curling her hand into a tight fist, she smashed it into his jaw and instantly regretted it.

Shaking her throbbing fist, Liz feared her attempt to knock him out would be the end of her. The guy's jaw was like rock, and when he grabbed her hands, she expected he would retaliate. When all he did was tie her back up, she stared at him with complete surprise.

"You'll have to hit me a hell of a lot harder than that, princess, to knock me out."

She watched as he carried the plate to the door, closing it and locking her in as he left. It baffled her that he hadn't done anything to her for her acting out. Surely the other guy would have smacked her back, yet this one hadn't even seemed fazed.

Hmmm, she wondered, and started working again on the ropes to break free.

Chapter 4

Tossing his mask on the counter, Mac set the plate in the dishwasher, then grabbed the towel hanging by the sink. Walking to the fridge, he grabbed the bag of ice from the freezer, set it on the counter, then grabbed a knife to open it.

"What are you doing?"

"Getting some ice." His jaw began to throb now. Who would have thought the woman could pack such a hardy punch?

"Why?"

Grabbing a handful of ice, Mac wrapped it in a towel then laid it on his chin. "She clipped me."

"What?" His blue eyes lifted to Mac's with surprise.

"She clipped me, right in the jaw. It wasn't much of a punch, but enough that I think it might bruise."

"She punched you?"

"I think I said yes."

"Shit. What did you do to her for that?"

Lifting his brow, Mac responded calmly. "I tied her up and left her sitting in the chair."

"You didn't hit her back?"

"No," Mac said, aghast. "Jesus, I don't hit women."

"Oh come on, you're telling me you've never hit a woman, not even once?"

"No, I have never hit a woman." And it didn't surprise him in the least that Terry condoned it. The guy was slime. He may look meek with his perfectly styled blonde hair and pretty boy face, but he'd heard stories about Terry's temper that worried Mac. That was why he didn't want him watching over Liz; he didn't trust the guy.

Terry made snorting noises as he waved his hands in disgust. "You're a wimp then. You gotta let the woman know who's in charge."

"You're unbelievable, Terry, you know that?" Leaving, Mac wandered outside with the ice on his chin.

He didn't hit women, and any man that did wasn't a real man in his opinion.

~

She might be glad he left the TV on for her, breaking the mundane silence, if he'd left it on something other than the sports channel. The sun had begun to set; she could tell that by the lighting in the room. She'd been here nearly an entire day so far and no one had come looking for her, which meant, she was stuck here.

Yeah, Liz, that's great, give up. Since when do you give up on anything? Struggling once more, she could feel the ropes around her body shifting, loosening. She was going to break free even if it meant skinning her wrists in the meantime.

She heard the door rattle and her heart skipped a beat. She hadn't heard anyone on the stairs, and when the door creaked open, her worst fears confirmed, as she watched Betty Rubble enter the room.

"Thought you might want some company."

He closed the door behind him, and she felt her heart hammering in her chest. She didn't trust him, didn't like him. He was the thinner of the two, yet he was the one that worried her the most.

"Cat got your tongue?" he said with a chuckle as he pulled a chair up right in front of her.

"What do you expect me to say?" She didn't want to say anything to him.

He shrugged thin shoulders, leaning forward to run his finger along her knee. "I don't know, you could tell me how much you want to get out of here."

Her skin crawled beneath the fabric of her slacks, and as his fingers slid higher on her thigh, she felt the nausea rolling in her gut. "I could pay you anything you like, just name the price." His eyes met hers and she saw beneath the mask that they were blue. She saw something else in his eyes and it sickened her. She knew just what he wanted and it had nothing to do with money, and when he ran his fingers along her thigh, up her hip, she felt the acid rise in her gut.

"The money sounds good, but I think we both know what I want from you."

She gulped hard, swallowing back the vomit rising in her throat as his hand cruised up and along her breast. "Please, don't do this."

"Oh, you know you want this as much as I do. I've read up on you, and I know just how many men you've let touch you." His hand slid to the buttons on her shirt, swiftly flicked one open, then the next.

Her entire body shaking, she knew she was going to be raped and there was nothing she could do to stop it. *Your legs are free, Liz, use them, fight, don't let him take you.* She felt his fingers skim over the swell of her breasts and she knew she needed to make her move. Lifting her leg, she rammed her foot right into his crotch.

"Fucking Christ." He buckled.

She saw the evil in his eyes through the mask when he lifted his head and the fear cut into her like a sharp knife. *Keep fighting, Liz, keep fighting.* "Keep away from me, you bastard." Kicking her feet, she caught him in the shins several times. When his fist came up, she wasn't quick enough to dodge it and felt the blow as it connected with her jaw. Liz saw stars before her eyes, felt the pain spear into her jaw and the nausea build in her belly.

"Stupid bitch, well, let's see how feisty you'll be while I'm pounding my dick into you."

She screamed when he yanked her slacks zipper down, screamed as he began to work the ropes to gain access to her. The next thing she knew the door flew open and Bart came charging into the room. For a brief moment she thought he, too, would have his turn with her, but then he grabbed the slime attacking her and threw him against the wall.

"What the hell are you doing?"

"The stupid bitch kicked me in the fucking dick, man."

"Get your ass downstairs, now." To insure he listened, Mac grabbed his shoulder and yanked him from the room.

The door slammed shut behind them, and Liz shook with the thought of what might have just happened. She could hear their voices through the closed door, heard the deep voiced one yelling. She didn't need to try to listen; his voice rang loud and clear through the closed door.

"You fucking bastard, you were going to rape her."

"I just wanted a little taste. She kicked me in the nuts, man."

"You fucking deserved that and more. You touch her again and I swear to God I will make damn sure you regret it. Got it?"

"Whatever."

She heard a hard thud against the wall and jumped.

"You lay one finger on her again and I'll make sure you never use that dick of yours again. Get out of my sight."

The door opened and Liz sucked in a breath, her body still shaking. He simply stood by the door, looking down at her. She heard him mumble something under his breath, then shake his head as he turned to the door and left.

Her lip quivered once, then once more before the tears fell from her eyes. She could taste the bile in her throat and swallowed several times to settle it back down. Her jaw throbbing, she knew her lip bled because she could taste the blood. Looking down at her opened clothing, the tears slid silently from her eyes.

Chapter 5

Mac didn't have a clue where Terry had gone off to, and he really didn't give a rat's ass. Just as long as the guy wasn't around him, or near Liz. He couldn't believe the bastard had been close to forcing himself on her. Grabbing the ice pack from the emergency kit, he gave it a snap to start the freezing process as he headed up the stairs for the antiseptic. Unlocking the bedroom door, he heard Liz sniffling and his heart sank. He didn't say a word as he moved towards her and took a seat in the chair across from her, lifting the ice pack to her mouth. When she jerked back, flinching, he wanted to kill Terry for making her so jittery. Scaring or hurting her hadn't been part of the plan.

"I'm sorry." Carefully he laid the bag against her mouth. "This will help the swelling." His eyes shifted to the open blouse and to the lush pink breasts, and his male hormones came to attention. Berating himself, he lifted his eyes.

"I...have some antiseptic here, to clean the wound to make sure it doesn't get infected." Setting the ice pack on the floor, he lifted the bottle, dabbing a cotton tipped swab in the solution. "He won't touch you again. I'll make sure of that." She winced when he touched the swab to her cut and he apologized once more. "Sorry."

He didn't blame her for not talking; her lip and jaw probably hurt like a bitch, and beyond that, she was probably utterly terrified. "Um...I'm going to untie you and let you...fix yourself up in the washroom." He stood, moving in behind her, and got busy untying the knots.

"There you go." Leaving the ropes on the floor, he took hold of her arm to help her up. He could feel her body shaking. He led her to the adjoining washroom near the window, stopping by the door. "I'll be waiting right here."

She caught the warning and entered the tiny washroom, closing the door behind her. She took one look in the mirror and her legs nearly buckled. With shaky hands she quickly did up the buttons on her blouse. She'd nearly been raped.

Feeling ill, she bent over the toilet and vomited until she emptied herself. Standing, she washed her mouth, then sat down and relieved herself. If the big guy hadn't come in when he had, she might have been—no, she *would* have been raped. She needed to get out of here, now. Looking around the tiny room, she threw the shower curtain open to see a tiny circular window that looked no bigger than her head. Damn it, so much for thinking she could escape from the bathroom.

She took a deep breath, gathering her strength, then pushed the door open. Seeing him waiting for her, she knew what she needed to do. With a quick lift of her leg, she kicked him hard in the gut, sending him stumbling backwards onto the bed. Dashing for the door, she yanked it open and let out a loud scream when he caught her around the waist. She wasn't beat yet, so she kept kicking and flailing with her arms.

"Jesus," he exclaimed as he tried to get a good hold on her. Wrapping his arms around hers, pinning them to her sides, he dragged her to the bed. It was then that he realized the ropes still lay by the chair. "Damn it."

"Let me go." Wiggling, trying to break free of his hold, she feared that now he, too, would take his turn with her. She saw the slimy bastard who attacked her enter the room and went completely still.

"What the hell is going on?"

"Get the ropes."

Her body stiffened momentarily when he climbed on top of her. "No, leave me alone; let me go; let me go." Liz grunted, fighting, trying to break his hold. The guy didn't just look big, he was big, and muscular. He felt like a lead weight pinning her down.

"Want me to tie her up?"

"No, just give me the ropes and go." He responded to Terry, then looked down at Liz with a thin smile. "Nice try, princess, you've got balls."

Relieved when Betty Rubble left the room, Liz let out a long breath. Then she felt her arms yanked above her head. Her pulse raced and her heart thundered as Bart tied her hands to the posts. "What are you going to do to me?" Was he going to punish her for trying to get away? *God, please, don't let him hurt me.*

"Tie you to the bed for one. Then I'm going to put some more ice on that lip."

Her brow furrowed in confusion. "Are you for real?"

"Last time I looked." He secured the knots, then lifted off of her to grab the ice.

"I just kicked you and tried to get away. I'd think you'd be pretty pissed at that." *What the hell is wrong with you, Liz? Stop egging him on!*

"Oh, I am." He laid the ice on her lip, his eyes meeting hers. "But I'm not going to smack you around for it. What the other guy tried to do to you, what he did do to you, I don't condone that sort of thing."

He was being serious, she could tell by the tone of his voice and the look in his eyes. "You're a baffling man—what's your name?" The bag of ice slid from her mouth as she spoke.

"Bart," he said with a smile, lifting the bag, holding it against her mouth.

"Right." *How droll.* "Then why are you doing this to me? Why not let me go?"

"I enjoy abuse," he said comically, as though trying to lighten her mood.

"Yeah, well, I'll be more than happy to give you all the abuse you like, Bart." She emphasized his name, her eyes narrowing with just a hint of humor in them.

"Pretty hard to do that, tied to the bed. Let's take a look at that lip." Pulling the ice from her lip, he leaned in to get a better look.

When his finger touched her bottom lip, she felt her breath catch.

"We'll just leave the ice on it a bit more." He stood, inhaling sharply.

"Where are you going?"

"Getting the lights."

"Why?" Her voice quivered.

"I told you, princess, I'm not like the other guy. It's getting late." He shut the light off and the only form of illumination came from the TV on the dresser.

"I really hate that name." She watched as he moved to the TV and shut it off. The darkness filled the room and her heart began to hammer. She felt the darkness surround her, smothering her with its greedy fingers.

"Yeah, why is that?" Clicking on the washroom light, he closed the door so that only a sliver of light could be seen.

She focused on the light, however small, and reminded herself there was nothing in the dark that could harm her. "I'm not royalty for one. What are you doing?"

With the light knitted blanket in hand, he draped it over her legs. "Covering you up?"

"Why?"

"In case you're cold during the night." Grabbing a pillow from beside her, he saw her eyes as they watched his every move. "Do you snore, princess?"

Her teeth gnashed again to the silly nickname. "No, I most certainly do not snore."

"We'll see. Sleep tight now." He carried the pillow to the arm chair in the corner beside the bed and tucked it behind his head as he sat down.

"You're sleeping here?"

"Yep. Don't let the bed bugs bite."

Rolling her eyes, she thought how childish that statement had been. She lay there tied to the bed fighting the sleep. She wanted to be on alert at all times, just to be safe, and every time he moved in the chair beside her, she waited, worrying, wondering. But inevitably sleep took hold and she dozed off.

Chapter 6

Her eyes shot open as the alarm clock buzzed beside her. "Shit." Her heart hammering, she watched as he reached over and shut it off.

"'Morning."

"It's only six o'clock." She yawned, her lip cracking and creating a ripple of burning pain. "Damn it."

"I'm an early riser. Hmmm, you opened it up some last night. Hurt much?"

"No, it feels wonderful, you idiot." She paused, shocked that she had said such a thing to him, and waited for any response, however brutal it might be.

"Well, someone's not very chipper in the morning."

She cocked her head to the side, baffled by his response.

"I guess I wouldn't be too chipper either if my lip was killing me. I'll clean it up for you, then grab some Advil for the pain."

She watched in complete astonishment as he walked to the washroom—he wasn't even disturbed with her? *Okay, what's up with this guy?* She needed to test the waters. "You try sleeping with your arms tied to the bed and see how happy you are in the morning."

He stepped from the washroom with a damp cloth, moving towards her. "I wasn't exactly comfortable either, princess."

Hmmm. "You could have slept in your bed. I didn't have a choice as to how or where I slept." She snarled her response, feeling rather brave now.

"Sweetie, you are in my bed." Leaning over her, he dabbed the blood on her chin.

Her pulse fluttered beneath her skin and as her eyes lifted to meet his, it fluttered even more. Sweet God, what the hell was wrong with her? How could she be feeling arousal from this man holding her captive?

"Liz?"

"What?" She jumped, her response quick.

"I asked if I let you go to the washroom to clean your lip, do you promise not to kick me again?"

She told her pulse to slow down, calmed her rapid breathing and nodded. She couldn't be feeling something for him, that was just...wrong.

"I can manage from here," she insisted as he hoisted her to her feet, trying to pull her hands from his. Her pulse fluttered again, and it pissed her off.

"I'm sure you can." But he helped her to the washroom just to be sure.

She closed the door in his face and turned to the mirror. Her face looked pale, her lip swollen and bloody, and her jaw hurt like a son-of-a-bitch. Her mind swirled with the arousal she felt being near him. She needed psychiatric help for lusting after her abductor. Splashing water on her face, washing her eyes, then carefully wiping her sore lip, she continued to think how idiotic it was to even think she could feel desire for him.

She did her business, ran her fingers through her hair trying to smooth it out as best she could without a brush, and opened the bathroom door. She saw Mac standing to the side, the ropes dangling in his hand. Her eyes lifted to his, then down to the ropes.

"Don't even think about it."

Making a break for it, she jutted to her right, then, faking him out, she bolted off to the left. She climbed over the bed, the blanket nearly tripping her up, then jumping off the bed, she ran for the door. She grabbed the door knob just as he came up behind her. She let out a squeal as he grabbed her left hand and pulled it behind her back, pinning her body to the door.

"Man, you just don't give up."

"Of course I'm not going to give up, you jackass. Do you think I'm just going to sit by and let you keep me tied up, for God sakes?" She jerked her body, trying to break free. He pinned her good and tight against the door. Her pulse began to flutter again, making her curse under her breath. When he reached in front of her to grab her right hand, she fought to keep him from taking it. Quicker than she was, he managed to grab it and pulled it behind her.

"And how did you expect to get out of here when the door is locked?"

"You didn't lock it last night when you came up to bed." He spun her around and pressed her against the door, holding her in place with his body. This time her pulse didn't just flutter, it hammered.

"Fine, so you would have made it out the door, then what? You wouldn't have gotten far, princess, with Betty Rubble keeping watch downstairs."

"At this hour, only a crazy person would be awake." She jerked her body once more, trying to get away from him. She felt pretty damn hot and it was getting very uncomfortable.

"Check it out, princess, you happen to be awake. Does that make you crazy?"

She knew she was panting but couldn't control herself. Being so near to him was making her pulse throb and her chest ache with need. "I didn't have a choice; your stupid alarm clock woke me." She lifted her knee, ready to strike.

Faster than she, he blocked her attempt with his hand. "I like the mornings."

"I like to sleep in."

Lost for words, they stared into each other's eyes, breathless. Moments passed before Mac shifted away, pulling her from the door. He didn't say a word to her as he led her to the chair. Knowing what he had planned for her now, she refused to allow it to happen. When he pushed her down into the chair, she stood right back up.

"Get a grip."

It shocked her when he lifted his leg and planted his knee on her chest. And when he leaned in closer to tie her up, she could smell his cologne, and it tickled her arousal. His hair beneath the mask brushed against her cheek as he bent near her ear to tie the ropes around her and it felt like satin. Turning her head, she saw the tufts of dark curly hair, and she nearly sighed.

"There, that should do it."

Liz sat in her chair as he left the room, her chest rising and falling with each heavy breath she took. "Oh my God, oh my God, oh my God." Letting her head fall back, she wasn't quite sure what to think. The man abducted her and was holding her captive, for God sakes, and she lusted after him. She didn't even know what he looked like, yet she wanted him. *God, Liz, get a grip.*

Coming to her senses, she realized she needed to get out, she just didn't know how. She'd tried to make a break for it, twice, only to be dragged back. The window, it was still her best chance, and the brief glances the night before led her to believe it would be plenty big enough for her to squeeze through. All she needed to do is break free of the ropes and she was set.

Shifting her body, she ignored the burning sensation the ropes caused as they rubbed against her skin. There would be plenty of time to sooth them when she broke free.

~

Feeling more himself after the cold shower, Mac headed for the kitchen to make some breakfast. Seeing Terry sitting at the table eating a plate of fluffy eggs soured his mood. Saying nothing to him, he moved to the fridge, grabbing the butter and jam. Setting them on the counter, he was pleased to see the coffee ready. Pouring himself a cup, adding a spoon of sugar, he pulled out the toaster and added four slices of bread, pressing the lever down.

"He called last night."

"What?" Mac turned sharply, the coffee in the cup sloshing over the rim to scald his fingers. Setting the cup on the counter, he put his fingers in his mouth. "Why didn't you come get me?"

Terry shrugged, lifting his own coffee cup to his lips, taking a sip before speaking. "Didn't want to disturb you."

"I'm in charge, Terry, you should have called me to the phone." He turned when the toast popped, annoyed. "What did he want?"

"He was checking in, making sure everything went smoothly. I told him everything went according to plan."

He buttered the toast then slopped jam on it. "What else?"

"That's it. Said he would be in touch."

Great, Mac thought, *he'd be in touch*. He had the easy part, while Mac put everything on the line. Not like he had much of a choice now, did he, and the guy knew that. Rock and a hard place, that's where he sat. Pouring another cup of coffee, he set both cups as well as the plate of toast on a tray then turned to the fridge and grabbed a bowl of strawberries, fresh from his own garden. "Tidy up for me while I'm upstairs okay."

"I'm not your bitch, Mac." Terry snarled into his cup.

"I didn't make the eggs, and thank you for sharing by the way."

"Whatever."

Clenching his jaw, Mac carried the tray up the stairs, wishing he didn't have to be stuck with the creep. But he'd had no choice in the matter, so he just had to put up with him.

Setting the tray on the floor, he pulled the key from his pocket, unlocked the door, then, pulling the mask from his back pocket, he slipped it over his head before opening the door. "Room service."

Her head shifted in his direction and her eyes focused on the tray in his hand. "Cheap restaurant if you call that breakfast."

"My, what a smart mouth we have, princess." Smiling, he set the tray on the bed and moved in behind her. "Right handed, right?" The scent of her hair tickled his nose and stirred his pulse.

"Yes."

Shaking it off, he untied her left hand then tied the right to the ropes around her body.

"I said I was right handed."

"I know." He took the plate of toast, lifted two pieces off the plate for himself, put a few strawberries beside hers then set the plate on her lap. "Here you go."

Liz looked down at the food before her, then back up at Mac. "You must have broken a sweat cooking for me. You shouldn't have."

Ooh, he loved her sarcasm. "All the more reason for you to enjoy it." He took a seat across from her, the tray on his lap with his toast and coffee.

"Where's my cup?"

"Over there." He motioned to the night stand, taking a bite of his toast.

She glanced to her left and saw the cup sitting there. "May I have it?"

"In time."

Her eyes shifted to his as her left eyebrow shot up. "Now what could I possibly do with a cup of coffee, aside from drinking it?"

"You strike me as the inventive type; you'd find other uses for it."

Her lip curled up but not enough to open the wound. "Like throwing it at you?"

"Bingo, princess."

"Afraid of me, big guy?" She bit into a strawberry, licking the juices that trickled from her mouth.

He watched her tongue as it lapped up the juices and felt his loins tighten. "Wary."

"Then why bring me a cup?"

His eyes were glued to the way she ate that luscious red juicy strawberry and the way her lips molded its form, the way her tongue lapped up the juices. "Why do you think it's sitting over there and not in your hands right now?"

Smiling, she licked the strawberry juice from her fingers. "And you think giving me a cooled cup of coffee is any better?"

He imagined his fingers in her mouth. "Cool coffee doesn't hurt as much."

"Ever had a cup smashed over your head?"

Shaking his mind clear, his eyes lifted to hers. "See, now that is exactly why I'm guarded." He stood now, knowing that if he didn't leave the room soon, he wasn't going to be able to. "Finished?"

"No."

"Then no coffee."

"Fine, I'm finished." She'd give up the last pieces of the overly sweet toast and juicy strawberries for the coffee any day.

"Here you go." Taking the plate, he set it on the tray with his coffee cup then walked to the door. "I'll be right back."

He closed the door behind him, locking it

Chapter 7

Some men were just not that bright; her abductor, apparently, was one of them. "You may be wary of me, but you certainly are stupid." Setting her coffee cup on the floor, she began untying herself. It didn't take her long to get the ropes off, even with her left hand, given the fact that she was ambidextrous. Grabbing the chair she'd been tied to, she waited by the door for him to return.

"You messed with the wrong woman, big guy." Giddy with excitement, she waited for him to return. She knew there would be no way she could get past him if she didn't knock him out, and she hoped the chair did the trick. When she heard his familiar steps coming towards her, she felt the excitement ripple inside of her. Lifting the chair as best she could, she grunted with its weight; then with great patience, she waited.

The keys jingled, the door knob turned, the door opened. The instant he entered the doorway, she sent the chair crashing down on him. With a hearty groan, he went down.

"Yes!" Jumping over him, Liz darted from the room, freedom in her sights. Though she hadn't knocked him out, she'd momentarily stunned him, which gave her enough time to make a break for it.

"She's loose," Mac called out, pushing the chair aside and bracing himself as he tried to stand.

She was free at last and nothing was going to prevent her from leaving. Seeing Betty Rubble blocking the bottom of the stairs didn't faze her; she lifted her foot and kicked him right in the face. Her bare foot sang with pain. Ignoring it, she jumped over his slumped body and searched for an escape. She'd have plenty of time to deal with the pain after she was free.

"Grab her," Mac yelled as he ran down the stairs.

"She fucking kicked me."

"Deal with it, she's getting away." Jumping over

Kidnapped

Terry's body at the bottom of the stairs, Mac ran after her.

She saw the back door and darted for it. Her hand reached out to the door knob as he caught up with her, grabbing her by the arm. She screamed, turning, fists ready.

Managing to avoid the fist flying towards his face, Mac grabbed her hand. "Son-of-a-bitch." His shin rang with pain from the blow from her foot.

"Let me go." She lashed out again, using her other hand to beat on his arms to get him to release her.

"The hell I will." Spinning her, he pinned her against the door. "Get over here and help me already."

Holding his bleeding nose, Terry swaggered towards Mac. "Just smack her, that'll calm her down."

"There's been enough hitting. Grab her legs when I turn her." Holding both arms behind her back, he spun them both and hooked one of his legs around hers to prevent her from booting Terry.

"You won't get away with this." Liz struggled, fighting to break free. When Betty grabbed her ankles, she bent her knees and tried pushing him away.

"Stupid bitch."

"Hold her," Mac warned him with stern eyes.

"I've got her."

"You'll pay for this, you bastards." Twisting her body wildly, she made it damn near impossible for them to hang on to her. They carried her back up the stairs and into the bedroom as she struggled. She finally managed to slip her hands free of Bart's hold, so she struck out at him and connected with Bart's jaw.

"Damn it."

"Yes, take that you bastard." Her victory was sort lived as he grabbed her hands in one of his, then released her body having her angling nearly to the floor.

"Get her to the bed."

"Now we're talking."

"No, no don't, please don't." Liz quivered; she knew

that tone in Betty's voice and she couldn't go through that again.

"Just grab the ropes."

The instant he set her on the bed, she tried to break free. Her breath hitched when he climbed on top of her, pinning her down. "You won't get away with this. I'll see you both burn in hell for what you've done to me." She bucked with her hips even though it was useless given the fact the guy weighed a great deal more than she did.

"Yeah, you keep dreaming, princess. Tie up her legs."

"Ouch," Liz gasped when Betty yanked her foot hard.

"Take it easy. There's no need to be rough, Betty."

"She fucking kicked me, Bart." Betty grabbed her other foot with as much force as he had the other.

"Get out of here, I'll deal with her. Go," Bart demanded.

"Whatever." Throwing his hands in the air, Betty shot Liz a nasty glare, then left the room.

"Now, let's get these hands of yours tied up."

"Get off of me, you brute." She bucked, trying to knock him off of her. He fell forwards, his head hitting hers. "Ouch."

"Very intelligent."

Her pulse began to flutter again and she felt her body react in the most pleasant of ways. They both stilled. Though she stared into the face of a silly cartoon mask, she saw the warm eyes behind it and felt herself lost in his gaze.

Holding her hands with one of his, he used the other to touch her bleeding lip. "You're bleeding," he said softly, his eyes shifting to meet hers.

"Oh," she sighed, lost in his gaze.

"I should clean it up for you."

"Uh huh," she panted, licking her lip. She tasted the blood and it drew her back. Blinking her eyes, breaking the hold he'd had on her, she came back to reality with a hard thud. "Get off of me already, you jerk."

"You've got a real smart mouth there, princess."

"And you're as heavy as an elephant." She bucked again, then remembered what happened the last time and settled down.

"If you had any weight on you, you might have been more successful in taking me out." He slid off of her and stood, looked down then quickly turned away. "I'll be right back with something for your lip."

The door closed and she heard him lock it from the other side. Blowing out a deep breath, Liz tried to get her system to level out. She felt hot, but it had nothing to do with the warmth of the room. She knew this feeling and it was not a comfortable one. She'd seen the bulge in his pants before he abruptly turned and hurried from the room, and lord it was doing a number to her system. How on earth could she be feeling desire? The guy was her abductor.

As she lay on the bed, her arms tied above her head, she wondered what it would have felt like if he'd kissed her.

~

Sifting through the medicine cabinet in the hallway washroom, Mac tried to get his mind off of Liz. There was something seriously wrong with him for wanting her. Number one, he was holding her captive, it was wrong to want her. Number two, she was so not his type. He didn't date prissy prima donna women. She wore designer everything and came from money and walked with her nose in the air, snubbing those beneath her—not the kind of woman who interested him.

Grabbing the skin glue, he reminded himself that in a few days it would all be over, she would go her way, he would go his. Liz would pass him sometime on the street and she wouldn't have a clue it had been him that had taken her. Sighing, Mac wondered if he would be able to forget her as easily. Lord knew the guilt nagged him, especially after Terry's attempted rape. His hand curled tight around the bottle. *Bastard.*

He needed to carry through with it; there was no other choice in that matter. Grabbing a cloth, he wet it, then walked back to the bedroom. In six days' time, he would hand the bank the money they demanded and he would have his farm, free and clear.

Yes, but at what price?

Chapter 8

She heard the key in the door and turned her head as he entered the room. Look at him, she thought to herself as she scanned her eyes over his body. He was big, his arms were muscular, his chest was wide, most likely as muscular as his arms, and he looked like a frikin' body builder. So not her type, not to mention the fact that he held her captive, for Christ's sake. Then how did he manage to turn her on? Yet when he approached, the scent of his cologne floating towards her, she felt her body stirring with need.

"I should have thought of this before."

Her mind clicked back. Looking up into that silly childish mask, she spoke without thought. "Perhaps thinking isn't your forte."

"Perhaps you should be grateful I'm fixing your lip," he snapped back, just as snide.

"Grateful, yes, I should be fucking grateful your buddy smacked me, splitting my lip. Jackass." She flinched, waiting for the assault.

Walking to the foot of the bed, he began untying her feet from the posts but leaving them tied together.

"What are you doing?" It astounded her that she constantly got away with the verbal abuse with him and never received any sort of repercussion.

"Moving you to the chair."

"You really are a glutton for punishment aren't you?"

He lifted her to her feet, holding her hands tight in his and met her glare. "I learn from my mistakes, princess."

"Stop calling me that." She spoke through gritted teeth.

"As long as it irritates you, *princess*, I'll keep using it. Let's go." His eyes narrowed with warning. "Don't even try it."

With a cocky smile, she yanked her hands free.

"And how far do you think you'll get with your hands

and your feet tied together?" Reaching out, he grabbed hold of her hands once more.

"I untied myself once, I'll do it again." She hopped as he pulled her towards the chair, creating as much resistance as possible.

"Only because I was stupid enough to leave you with one hand untied." He pushed her down onto the chair.

"At least we both agree you're stupid."

His hands holding her against the chair, he leaned down and got right in her face. "You really are gutsy for someone being held against her will."

Her chin jutting out, she retorted. "You don't scare me, Bart."

"I could change that very easily."

One look in his eyes and she knew better. He may look big, but he didn't scare her in the slightest. "Is that Calvin cologne? I love the scent, very soft, very...non-threatening." She gritted her teeth in a mock smile.

His teeth grinding, he grabbed the ropes and began winding them around her body.

"Got nothing to say to that, do you, big guy?"

"You know, I still have the gag we used on you and I'm not against using it again."

"You wouldn't dare," she challenged.

With a devious smile, he walked to his dresser, pulled open the top drawer and grabbed a red hanky. Turning to her, he waved it in her face. "Oh, I dare."

"I'll scream."

"No one will hear you."

She'd see about that. As she opened her mouth, ready to scream, she realized her mistake. He shoved the cloth in between her teeth, then tied it behind her head.

Laughing, he moved around to face her, dusting his hands. "Still in control here, princess, best to remember that."

"Jackass," she mumbled through the cloth, furious.

Still laughing, he opened the door and left her to fume.

"What was that all about?" Terry asked as Mac came down the stairs.

"Me having a little fun."

"So why is it okay for you to have fun but I can't?"

Mac turned to him with a frown. The guy was unbelievable. "Because my kind of fun doesn't involve assault. Make something for dinner, okay?"

"I'm not your bitch, Mac, do it yourself."

"What the hell is your problem?"

"I'm bored of this shit already."

"Fine, then leave." Nothing would please him more if the guy walked.

"I'm in this just as much as you, Mac, and I'm not leaving until I get what's mine." Terry stood, challenging Mac.

"What? An acting gig? Like that's reason enough to kidnap someone." Mac snorted, pulling out a cigarette and lighting it.

"A lead role," Terry corrected, "and let's discuss why you're doing it, Mac. Because your daddy couldn't afford to make the payments on this place before he died."

Mac's fist curled at his side but he didn't use it, even though he wanted to smash it into the bastards face. "Make something for dinner," he said through gritted teeth. Yes, his father hadn't been able to make the payments, but only because his health had been failing and he hadn't wanted his sons to know.

"What the hell am I supposed to make?" Sitting back down, Terry picked up his journal and began writing.

"There's chicken in the fridge, cook it however you see fit. I'll be upstairs watching after Liz." He crushed his cigarette out in the ashtray with a great deal of force.

"Why don't you cook and I'll watch her?"

"Because I don't trust you to even look at her. Do as I tell you."

His back up, Terry stood once more. "Who the fuck do

you think you are?"

"I'm the guy who's not telling the boss what you tried to do, and you know if he found out, you would be out on your ass without that lead role, or any fucking role for that matter. Still want to challenge me, pal?"

Gritting his teeth, Terry sat down and went back to his journal.

"Didn't think so." Enjoying his victory, Mac headed back up the stairs.

Chapter 9

The instant he entered the room, Mac saw the contempt in Liz's eyes. Closing the door behind him, Mac walked casually towards her. "You don't look happy, princess. I wonder why that is?" He paused in front of her, his hands reaching behind her head. "Want me to untie this for you?"

The look she gave him could have sent any man running for cover. Mac thought how fortunate he was that he had the upper hand.

Smirking, he untied the gag. Slipping it from between her lips, he saw the dried blood and berated himself for being so inconsiderate. "I'll clean that up for you now." Taking the gag, he walked to the washroom and grabbed a cloth, running warm water over it before returning. "My, we sure are quiet now."

"I was always told that if I didn't have anything kind to say to not say anything."

Pulling the chair closer, Mac sat down and began dabbing the cut. "Where was that thinking when you called me names earlier?"

His hands were gentle as they wiped the cut. "Momentary lapse." She hissed when he ran the cloth over the cut, opening it.

"Sorry."

"What kind of abductor apologizes?"

With nothing to say to that, he pulled the glue from his pocket and held it up for her to see. "This is skin glue. I should have used it right off the bat but I wasn't thinking. It'll seal the cut and prevent it from opening and help it heal faster. It won't hurt."

"You have need for skin glue often?" she asked as he opened the bottle and pulled the dropper out.

"Often enough."

"Then you've used it on your victims before?"

His eyes met hers and the guilt trickled inside of him. "No, you're my first."

"Oh really, I never would have guessed." Her comment was snide.

"You know, I could just as easily use this glue to seal up that smart mouth of yours," he warned with marked precision.

"You don't have the balls to do that."

She was right, he wouldn't do that to her, but she didn't have to know that. "Don't push me, princess. Now be a good girl and open your mouth so I can fix your lip."

Snarling, she opened her mouth, shooting daggers with her eyes.

"Good girl." He applied a thin layer of glue to the crack, then waved his hand over it to help it seal. "I wouldn't close your mouth for a few seconds yet, unless you want it sealed shut."

She didn't respond but simply narrowed her eyes even more.

Closing the bottle, he took it along with the cloth back to the washroom. Returning to the room, he clicked on the TV and turned his chair to watch.

"What are you doing?"

"Watching TV. I thought I told you to not talk for a bit and let the glue dry."

"It's dry. Why are you watching TV in here?"

His arms folded over his broad chest, he kicked his legs out and got comfortable. "What's the matter, you don't want my company?" He turned to her and a glimmer of humor shone in his eyes through the mask.

"You're only here because you're worried I'll try to make another break for it."

"Right on the nose, princess." Lifting the remote control, he flicked through the channels.

Fine, he wanted to keep an eye on her? She had some questions for him in that case. "So, big guy, what's the asking price for me?"

"I've already told you not to worry about that." He stopped on the Discovery Channel and watched as two divers fed fish to a shark. Pretty damn gutsy, he decided, and something he would never have the nerve to do.

"Why? What's the big deal if I know what you're asking for me?" She tried to shift in the chair, her butt falling asleep and making it uncomfortable to sit still.

"Why do you need to know?" He pulled his cigarette pack from his pocket and lit one up.

"Maybe I can match it."

He laughed, tipping his head back, smoke escaping from his lips. "Sure you can."

"I have money," she justified, her chin jutting out.

"Is that so? And how do you have this money? Do you have a job?"

Her jaw tightened. "No."

"No, didn't think so. You live off of Daddy's money." He blew a cloud of smoke in the air above his head, then tapped it out in the ashtray sitting on the dresser.

Her eyes narrowed. "And where will this money be coming from that you—I assume— have asked for my safe return? My father, perhaps?"

Touché. "I still have the gag, sweetheart," he warned her evenly.

"I just want to know what you're asking for my return. She paused, swallowing her fear. "You don't intend to ask for money and your intentions are to kill me."

It bothered him that she would even think such a thing. "If that were the case, princess, would I be sitting here taking your abuse? I don't think so."

"Then why are you being so obstinate about telling me the amount you're asking for me?"

Letting out a long breath, he turned to her. "Fine, you want to know how much, princess? I'll tell you. One hundred billion dollars." He snickered.

She snorted, rolled her eyes. "What a moron."

"Hey, I'd watch what you say to me. Remember I'm the one in charge here and I can make your life hell."

"Oh yes, but then you'll apologize for it afterwards.

Ooh, I'm terrified."

"See this, it's my trusty friend Mr. Hanky, and he's looking forward to getting to know your teeth a little better." He waved the hanky in the air.

"How sad for you that your only friend is a worn out looking piece of cloth."

"That's it, it's going back on." The knock on the door made him growl. Grabbing the door, he thrust it open and glared at Terry.

"Dinner." Terry shoved a tray out to Mac with a great deal of force.

Taking it, Mac chose not to acknowledge his attitude and shut the door in his face. One look at the food indicated the lack of effort the guy had put into making it. "Dinner time, princess."

He set a plate of chicken and mashed potatoes on her lap, and as she examined it, she spoke. "Wow, not only do you mend my cuts but you feed me such enticing meals. I am the luckiest hostage ever."

"Hey, I could just as easily take it back, princess," Mac challenged, reaching out to take the plate.

"That's fine, I'll eat it."

Stepping around her, he knelt down to untie her right hand. "Don't make me regret this."

She pulled her free hand away from his touch and gave it a twist. "How am I supposed to eat this without utensils?"

"It's chicken, you're meant to pick it up with your fingers. Or is that too low class for you princess?"

She snarled, responding in kind. "Chicken can be eaten with your fingers, dumb ass, but not the mashed potatoes." Scooping some on her finger, she daringly flicked it towards his masked face.

His brow lifted beneath the mask, and he admired her boldness. "If you're hungry enough, you'll use your fingers." Wiping it from his mask, he flicked it towards her, hitting her right on that upturned nose of hers.

Aghast, she scooped up the potatoes on her plate and threw them smartly at his face. "Be my guest."

He blinked with surprise, then decided two could play that game and scooped the potatoes from his face and threw them back at her, laughing at the shock on her face. "Okay, truce." He held his hand up when he saw the look in her eye. "Let me help you clean that off your face."

"I can manage, just give me a napkin." Scooping what she could feel from her face, she flicked her hand, the potatoes flying towards him. "Oops, I'm sorry."

"Like hell you are." He decided it might be best to let it go. Standing, he grabbed the napkins from the tray and handed a few to her. "Sure you don't want me to help?"

"I can manage, thank you." She took the napkins and began to wipe her face.

"You missed a spot, right…there." He touched the side of her nose, his eyes meeting hers.

"Thank you." Her eyes still on his, she wiped the spot he'd touched.

"Here." Taking her hand in his he felt her pulse fluttering as he guided her to the spot she'd missed. He helped her wipe her face, his eyes never leaving hers. Then her tongue slid from her mouth to lap up the potatoes from her lips and he felt it hit him directly in the loins. God, what he wouldn't give to feel that tongue on his— "There, you've got it now." Uncomfortable, he sat down, setting his plate on his lap.

They sat in silence, eating the flavorless chicken, neither sparing the other a look. The heat that stirred between the two of them was obvious, and neither knew how to deal with it. Silence remained as he gathered up their dishes and left the room.

Chapter 10

She couldn't say the meal had been satisfying, as it had been tough and flavorless. The potatoes, what hadn't landed on her face, had been just as bland. But she wasn't hungry, not for food. Her appetite seemed to turn to a more primitive sort of desire, and that desire happened to be directed towards her abductor.

She couldn't understand why she felt anything for him, yet it was obvious her body reacted to being near him, to his touch. She remembered a condition in which the abducted became infatuated with their abductor. What was it called again… Stockholm Syndrome, that was it, that's what she suffered from. It was understandable, considering, she was near Bart the most. And when Betty attempted to rape her, Bart came to her rescue. He even mended her wounds.

Okay, now that she'd identified it, she felt marginally better. The best thing for her would be to get the hell out of here and fast. But how? Her attempt to knock him out and escape failed miserably. So now what?

She heard a vehicle in the distance through the window, driving on what sounded like a gravel road. If she could hear traffic, there had to be people around. Moving her hands quickly, she tried to loosen the ropes. It would take forever to get untied and by that time, he would be back. She needed another plan. *Think, Liz, think.* She tapped her toes as her mind worked.

Her feet. Sure they were tied together, but she could still move them. If she played her cards right, she could do this. Taking a deep breath, she pushed her upper body from the chair, leaning forward. The chair rocked but not enough for her to be able to stand up. So she pushed a little harder next time. Working up a sweat, she rocked herself back and forth, the chair teetering backwards worrying her that it might fall. Then where would she be? Screwed is where. One more time, she thought, and gave it one good thrust. Rocking forward, she planted her feet and hoisted herself up. She staggered, the chair a heavy weight on her back, but she managed to stand. "Yes," she cheered, then silenced herself, waiting for any sounds that they might have heard her. Relieved when she didn't hear him, she bounced on her feet. Bent at the waist, her hands tied behind the chair, she turned, trying to face the window. Working up quite a sweat, she began to hop towards it. Freedom her reward.

Her foot caught on the bed cover, tripping her. She tried to right herself, but knew it was too late. As she began to fall face first to the floor, her only thought was damn it, she'd been so close.

~

Mac heard the crash and bolted for the stairs, slipping the mask over his face, snagging the key from his front jeans pocket. Quickly unlocking it, he thrust the door open, and saw the chair, Liz and all, tipped over at the foot of the bed, near the bathroom door. "Jesus." He rushed to her, ready to lash out. "What the hell were you doing?" But as he approached her, he saw her head twisted at an odd angle and he could tell she'd been knocked unconscious.

"Shit. Liz, Liz, can you hear me?" he tapped her face, panicking. "Come on, Liz, talk to me." When she still didn't respond, he called down to Terry for help.

"What's going on?" Rushing into the room, Terry saw the chair with Liz still in it, tipped over.

"I don't know, she…fell. Help me get her untied." He worked fast to untie her, wondering what the hell she had been up to.

"Fell, all the way over here?"

"I don't know, okay, just untie her. Liz, come on princess, speak to me."

As Mac removed the ropes, her body slid to the floor. Scooping her up, he pushed the chair aside, lifting her in his arms with no effort what so ever, and carried her to the bed. "Get me a cold cloth."

Hurrying to the washroom, Terry grabbed the cloth lying in the sink and wet it with cold water. "Here."

Mac took it and swiped it across her face. "Come on Liz, wake up. Shit, she's got a welt on the side of her head."

"The boss ain't gonna like that."

Where'd that sort of thinking been when he'd decked her in the first place? "I don't give a shit about that right now. Come on, Liz, honey, wake up."

"Hmmm," Liz murmured, her eyes still closed.

"That a girl, come on, wake up now." He stroked the cloth across her cheeks, relieved when he saw her eyes flutter open.

"Crap."

"Stay with me now."

"What…where am I?"

He watched with utter relief as her eyes fluttered open. "On the bed. Can you tell me what your name is?"

"Rumplestiltskin."

He wasn't sure if she'd been joking or not so he asked again. "I need you to tell me your name."

"Oh, for Christ's sake, it's Liz, happy? Damn, my head hurts."

Mac turned to Terry. "Go to the medicine cabinet down the hall and grab the bottle of Advil and some water."

She startled him when she bolted upright, and as she tried to swing over the bed, he saw that Terry had left the door open. He pressed her back down onto the bed, shaking his head. "What the hell is wrong with you?"

"You, you're what's wrong with me."

"Close the door next time," Mac berated Terry the instant he entered the room. "She tried to make a break for it."

He held the bottle and the glass of water out to Mac, snarling. "How the hell was I supposed to know that? She doesn't look very mobile. Here."

Mac took the bottle and the glass, glad when Terry left the room, this time closing the door behind him. "Here, these should help."

She took the pills he held out to her, then the water and washed them down.

"Now, you wanna tell me what the hell you were doing?"

"Practicing ballet."

"Well your attitude's back, that's a good sign. Now, the real reason?"

"I was trying to get to the window,"

"How exactly did you plan on doing that?" When he saw her eyes closing he snapped his fingers in her face. "Stay with me here, Liz."

"I am awake, and stop snapping your fingers. I pushed myself forward enough so I could walk to the window."

"Tied to the chair?"

"Yes."

He would have liked to have seen that. "And the purpose for the little adventure?"

"I wanted some fresh air," she replied dryly. "Figure it out, ace."

She certainly had an attitude. "Sweetheart, if you planned on escaping from that window, you'd have had a long fall."

"Is that supposed to deter me?"

He bit back a grin and for the first time since he'd taken her captive, she impressed him.

"Well, then, I guess I know what I have to do." Grabbing her hands, he lifted them above her head and began tying them to the bed posts.

"What are you doing?"

"Tying you up."

"Come on, I think I've already proven I can't go far."

"I have to leave the room for a minute, think I'm going to leave you untied?" He snorted a laugh. "I think not. Try not to do anything stupid while I'm gone."

"Try not to do anything stupid while I'm gone," she mimicked him in a snotty tone.

Laughing, Mac closed the door, locking it behind him.

Chapter 11

Still smiling, Mac came down the stairs, tucking the mask in his back pocket. He found Liz's snide attitude amusing and her gutsiness admirable. Despite her idiocy for trying to escape while bouncing in her chair, she could have seriously hurt herself. He felt an uneasy sensation in the pit of his belly that had nothing to do with worry over what the boss would say and more to do with his own feelings. He'd actually been concerned for the stupid fool, what had she been thinking? *Trying to get away from you, dumb ass.*

"Where are you going?"

"To get my tools."

"What for?"

"She'd been going for the window, I need to seal it."

"Get out!"

Shrugging, Mac stepped out into the dark night and walked across his property to the garage. He gave her credit; at least she tried everything in her power to get free. It was the last thing he expected from her. The woman looked like a typical girly girl who would cry at the drop of a hat and didn't do anything strenuous. She had people for that sort of thing.

Grabbing the drill, a few screws and the security bars that had once been on the basement windows, he headed back to the house. He passed Terry without a word and took the steps by twos. She wasn't going to be getting away anytime soon.

Opening the door, drill under his arm, bars in his hand, he saw Liz on the bed, her golden hair fanned out beneath her on the dark blue pillow, her eyes closed. Setting the bars and tools down on the floor by the window, he walked to her, placing a hand on her cheek. She jumped, making him jump.

"What?"

"Just checking."

"Checking what?"

"I just wanted to make sure you weren't out cold again."

"I'm fine," she snapped, closing her eyes to the pain.

Shaking his head, Mac grabbed the drill and the bars and pushed the curtains aside.

"What are you doing?"

"Nervous, princess?"

"Hardly. Are you putting up bars?"

"Yep." Lifting the drill, he inserted a screw, then pressed the switch. Frowning, he looked at the drill, baffled as to why it wasn't working.

"Problem?"

"I'll figure it out." He gave it a shake, frowning.

"Maybe you should try plugging it in first."

"I did plug it in." He gave it another shake, pressing the button several times.

Her eyes darted to the dangling cord and the fact that it wasn't attached to the wall. "No, you didn't."

"Yes, I did."

"Then why isn't it attached to the wall?" she asked mockingly.

"Look, princess, I think I know how to work a tool." But as he turned, he saw that he hadn't plugged it in. *Great, you fool.*

"Told you so."

Growling under his breath, he inserted the plug into the wall. Lifting his head, he shot her a brazen smile, then turned it on.

"Jackass," she called out to him over the noise.

"Sorry, can't hear you."

"Imbecile."

Whistling, he inserted the screw once more, and went to work attaching the bars. He clicked it off after finishing and set the drill down.

"Thank God."

"Was that loud, princess?"

"You know, a little concern for my head injury would

be nice."

He lowered his head, feeling like a heel for not being more concerned. Setting the drill aside, he sat on the bed and leaned in close, taking a look at her head.

"What are you doing?"

"Checking out your head."

"Why don't you get a little closer?"

"Your sarcastic wit astounds me, princess." She amazed him with her smart mouth, given her situation.

"Well, excuse me for not being in a joyful mood. If you wanted me docile, you should have drugged me."

The woman was unbelievable. "Oh, there's still plenty of time for that."

"Yeah, then what are you waiting for?"

"Jesus, you're pretty fucking nervy." His fingers clenched around her head.

"You haven't seen anything yet, big guy," she challenged, her chin jutting out.

"Bring it on, sister," he challenged, his eyes drifting to her luscious lips.

Paused in the moment, passion stirring between them, their eyes locked on lips that wanted and needed. The only sounds in the room were the labored pants of their breath.

"I..."

"Hmmm...?"

She closed her eyes, anticipating, opening her mouth ever so slightly.

He leaned in closer, felt her breath against his lips, saw the cut on hers, and he paused. What the hell was he doing? "I should clean this up." Pushing from the bed, feeling keyed up and bitter with himself, he scooped up the drill. This hadn't been in the game plan. It seemed so damn simple. Grab the girl, hold her for a week, then get paid enough money to pull your home out of debt. Wanting the woman in question hadn't been in the plan.

Chapter 12

Liz watched as he gathered up the drill, shifted the curtains back into place, then marched over to the door. Her body was still on fire and her mind reeling. Oh how she wanted him to kiss her, she would have given herself willingly the instant their lips had touched.

And then what, Liz? Do you think for one moment he would let you go simply because you had sex with him?

The click of the door surprised her back to reality and turning, she saw him pull up a chair and take a seat. "What are you doing?"

"Watching TV." He flicked through the channel and gave an appreciative hmmm when he found a boxing match to watch.

Closing her eyes, she listened to the muffled sounds of padded fists hitting flesh. It was beyond her why any man would subject himself to such torture. It would figure that he would take an interest in such a barbaric sport; he had the physique for it. It made her wonder if he might be a boxer.

And that sent her imagination soaring. He would wear a pair of black satin shorts, to match his hair, fitting quite nicely to his tight round ass. She was human, after all; she noticed it. His muscles would bulge with every jab, glistening with sweat from his exertion. The dark hair on his chest—she was sure he would have hair on his chest—would cling to his damp sweaty skin. God, he would look hot, dancing back and forth, his gloved hands held high, ready for the fight.

"Liz, you okay?"

She jerked back to reality with a hard thud, blinking several times as her mind tried to separate fantasy from reality. "I'm fine."

"Are you sure? You look a little flushed."

"I said I was fine; go back to your stupid boxing game." She blew air over her face to cool down.

"Match," he corrected. "Excuse me for being concerned."

"Match, game, same damn thing." She tried to shift, the pain in her shoulder shocking her, making her wince.

"What?" Worried, he turned to her and saw the discomfort in her face. "You okay?"

"No, damn it, I'm not okay. My frickin' shoulder is killing me."

Setting the remote on his chair, he stood and moved to the bed. "Let me take a look." He reached out to her shoulder; she jerked it away, wincing. "Liz, trust me, I just want to have a look."

That sounded ridiculous, coming from the man who'd abducted her. Yet when Liz looked up, her eyes meeting his, something told her she could trust him with her life. "Okay."

"Does that hurt?"

"A little, yeah." His hand on her shoulder felt so gentle that she closed her eyes and relaxed. He really did have nice hands.

"Okay, try rotating it?"

Lifting her shoulder, she moved it, wincing.

"That's a good sign, you can move it." His hand caressed her shoulder tenderly. "You probably bruised it when you fell. I'll get—Betty to bring up my heating bag. It's one of those rice filled bags you can heat or freeze and isn't as constricting as the ones you plug into the wall."

"Hmm?" His hand felt incredible, warming her body, making her heart beat in quick jerky movements, her pulse drumming in time with her head. She hadn't heard a word he had just said.

"Liz?"

"Hmm."

Cocking his head to the side, his lips curved up with a faint smile. "Does that feel good?"

"Yes." Sliding her head over, she welcomed the hands that slid along her shoulder, soothing the ache.

"Want me to give you a massage, princess?"

The name he called her brought her back. Opening her eyes, she responded. "That would be nice, but you would have to untie me first."

Laughing, pulling his hand free, he stood. "Good one, princess, you almost had me. How stupid do I look? Don't," he warned her, his index finger held up.

She gave him a look that clearly told him she wasn't going to listen to him. "Oh, where do I begin?"

"You don't."

She laughed a quick frivolous laugh. "Well, for one, you look ridiculous smoking with that silly child's mask on your face, and let's not forget how you tripped over your own laces, and the fact that you forgot to plug in the drill before using it. Oh, no, you aren't stupid at all."

She could see his eyes narrowing through the holes in his mask and grinned proudly.

"And you're so smart, princess? Let's not forget why you're laying on that bed with a lump on your head and a sore shoulder."

"Because you abducted me and tied me to a God damn chair," she spat back.

"Because you so stupidly thought you could move while tied to that chair."

"Right, like I'm going to sit by while you keep me here and play miss damsel in distress. *Oh my, what will I do, help me help me, I'm a helpless little woman.*" She snorted, rolling her eyes. "Jackass."

"You look pretty damn helpless now, lying in the bed, tied to the posts. Hmm, I wonder who the victor is? Wait, that's me." Laughing, he turned to the door.

Snarling, Liz fumed as he left the room, leaving her tied to the bed.

Chapter 13

The clock on the bedside table read just after nine. Great, time really flies when you're having fun. And her damn nose had been driving her nuts for the past fifteen minutes. Turning her head, she rubbed her nose on her shoulder and winced when that small move caused her pain.

The sound of heavy footsteps leading to her door gave her pause for a moment, then she went back to rubbing her nose against her other arm.

Mac stepped into the room just at that moment and paused as he watched her head bobbing back and forth. "Got a problem?"

"My nose is itchy. How else was I supposed to scratch it?"

"I hate when that happens and your hands are tied up and you can't reach it." He paused for effect. "Wait, my hands are free." He laughed as he held his hands up and waved them in the air.

"You're a riot." She snorted and turned her head away from him.

"I know, I'm a walking joke—don't even think about it."

"That one was just too easy. What are you doing?" she asked cautiously when he reached out to her hand.

"Letting you go to the washroom." He undid the last knot and freed her, holding her hands in his, securing her.

"You're too kind," she replied dryly, then sat up slowly; she didn't much care for the room spinning.

"I know, I'm all heart."

Shooting him a nasty glare, she made her way the whole three feet to the washroom and closed the door behind her. Her head throbbed something fierce, her shoulder ached and she felt as if she might vomit. She did her business, breathing through the nausea and dizziness. Standing, she did herself up and felt the room swirling around her. Oh, not a good feeling.

Grabbing hold of the sink, she turned on the cold water, hoping the coolness would make her feel better. Her vision began to distort and darken and she felt her legs give out. She slid to the floor as everything went black.

~

Mac heard a faint thud and moved up to the door. "Liz? Liz?" He could hear the water running, so why wasn't she answering him? "I'm coming in, Liz." Turning the door knob, he opened the door. It hit something and when he looked down, he saw her legs. "Crap." Slipping through the tiny opening in the doorway, he slid down beside her crumpled body lying up against the vanity. "Come on, baby, wake up."

"Hmm."

Scooping her up, he carried her to the bed. Laying her down, he sat beside her, stroking her face. "Come on, sweetheart; open those big green eyes of yours."

"Oh...I don't feel so well."

"Okay, just keep your eyes closed. I'll get you some water." Leaving her untied, he walked to the washroom, pulled a paper cup from the dispenser and filled it with water. "Liz?" he called to her as he moved back towards the bed.

"Yeah," she murmured, her voice sluggish.

"I'm going to help you sit up so you can drink some water, okay?"

"Sure."

"Here you go." He held the cup to her lips when she opened her eyes.

She took a few sips, then pushed the cup aside. "Thanks."

"Sure." He set it on the bedside table, then brushed the hair from her face with his hand. "Feeling any better?"

"A little. I'm tired." Her words slurred as she drifted off to sleep.

He held her against his chest, stroking the silky hair from her face, and the realization of what he took part in cut a deep wound in his heart. What made him think he could abduct another human being for his own gain and all would be well? She was suffering, Terry had beaten the crap out of her, tried to have his way with her and now she was feeling sick from a fall that wouldn't have happened if he hadn't have taken her captive.

Well, enough was enough.

Sliding out from beneath her, he laid her head gently on the pillow, then covered her with the blankets. She looked like an angel, the way she slept, and it made his decision all the easier. He closed the door behind him then moved down the stairs.

"How's she doing?" Terry asked.

"She's sick. Where's the phone" Seeing it on the counter, he picked it up, checked the number on the note pad by the phone.

"What are you doing?"

"Ending it."

"What?"

"Hello, it's me. It's over." He spoke into the phone, his voice determined.

"*What's happened? I told you only to call this line in an emergency,*"

"It is." Mac couldn't tell the guy everything that had happened, but he could tell him some of it. "She's sick."

"*She'll be fine.*"

"No, she won't. I want this to stop. I'm calling it off."

"*You will do as I say and you will carry through with this. Understood?*"

"But—"

"*No, you agreed to do this and you will carry through with it. Remember why you're doing it, Tyrell. Three more days.*"

Listening to the buzzing on the other end, Mac fumed. Slamming the phone down on the counter, he turned and saw Terry standing behind him. "What?"

"You can't quit now, Mac, come on. She'll be fine,

and in a few days, this will all be water under the bridge."

Fuming, Mac stomped back up the stairs. Yes, water under the bridge for them, but what about for Liz?

Chapter 14

He hadn't slept much during the night. It wasn't just that he left Liz untied on the bed all night that worried him, it was the fact that she seemed so ill the previous evening. It worried him when she'd blacked out; it sickened him that he still carried through with it. His thoughts weighed heavily on him during his sleepless night, and his conscience was telling him to just say to hell with it, pick her up, carry her to the car, and take her home.

But then he'd looked around the room and he saw what he would be losing if he did. His home, his family's home, the place his parents had struggled to raise three obstinate boys and push them towards a better life then they'd had. And for the most part, they'd succeeded. But even his job as a stunt double wasn't enough to save his family home. He had a car loan; he just couldn't understand why the bank wouldn't give him another loan to pay off the rest of the mortgage.

He looked over at Liz as she lay curled up on his bed. She looked as if she belonged there, resting on his pillow, but he knew better. A few more days and it would all be over and behind him. Well, the first day and a half had been a horror for her; maybe he could make the rest of her time here a bit better.

"Liz, Liz, I need you to wake up."

"Go away." Waving him off with her hand, she curled into the pillow.

Well, he needed a shower and he couldn't leave her untied on the bed while he wasn't in the room, and he damn well wasn't going to trust Terry to watch over her. Left with no other option, Mac grabbed the ropes, and moved to the bed. Closing his eyes and sighing, regretting having to do it, he took hold of her hand.

"What are you doing?" she asked groggily, her eyes peering open through slats.

"Tying you up. How do you feel?"

Opening her eyes, she looked around the room, a little baffled. "What do you mean, tying me up? I was untied all night?" She sat up, looked around

"Well, you seem clear headed. Maybe the chair instead of the bed."

She jerked her hand from his and slid from the bed. "I'll tell you where you can shove that chair, pal." She teetered, bracing herself on the bed.

"I'm sure you could, but you might want to wait until you're feeling better. Maybe it would be best to leave you tied to the bed."

"I could think of several things I could do with those ropes where you're concerned."

"Ooh, nasty today, aren't we?" Tugging her down onto the bed, he could tell she wasn't herself or she would have put up more of a fight. He tied her right hand to the post, then crawled over her and tied up the other. "I'll be back in a half an hour with breakfast."

"Can't wait."

Locking the door behind him, picking up the drill, and removing his mask, Mac headed down the stairs. He could smell a heavenly aroma and let his nose lead the way. "What's this?" Mac sniffed the fluffy golden eggs smothered in cheese cooking in the pan.

"I decided to make breakfast."

"Why?" His last encounter with Terry, the guy hadn't been too pleased with the fact that Mac had wanted to end it all…ah…now he got it. Well, if this is what he got for threatening to quit, maybe he would make the threat more often.

"Felt like it. Hope you like it."

"I'm sure we will." Grabbing two plates, Mac scooped some into each plate, grabbed a slice of toast for each then set them on the tray.

"I didn't…you're bringing her some?"

"Of course I am." Pouring two cups of coffee, adding a spoon of sugar to his, he set them on the tray as well then went in search of his plastic cutlery. "Why wouldn't I?"

"She tried to get away again."

"So you want me to punish her by not feeding her?" Mac pulled his head out of the pantry, shooting Terry a nasty look. "I don't work that way. Clean this up, will you, I want to take a shower when I'm done breakfast."

Carrying the tray on his hip, Mac pulled the key from his pocket as he took the steps up. He slipped the mask back over his head, then unlocked the door and stepped inside. "Breakfast is served."

The scent of coffee and eggs aroused her hunger and opening her eyes she saw the tray he held. "Smells good."

"Looks good, too."

"That was a fast shower. You don't believe in changing your clothing?"

"I was distracted by food; I'll take one after breakfast." Setting the tray on the bed, he began loosening the ropes just enough so she could sit up and use her hand, but not enough to be able to untie herself. "There you go." He set the tray with her plate and cup on her lap, then sat on the bed with his.

"Aren't you going to untie the other one?" She gave her hand a tug.

"Nope."

"It's not exactly easy to eat this way." She struggled to pick up the fork.

"Life's rough."

"*Life's rough*," she mimicked in a snotty tone, picking at her eggs.

"Well, your smart mouth doesn't seem to have been affected. How's the head?" he asked as he lifted a forkful of eggs to his mouth.

"Throbbing like a bitch."

"That'll teach you to pull a stupid stunt."

Her eyes narrowed in on him as she lifted her fork and aimed it at him. "Keep pissing me off, big guy, and you'll be wearing an eye patch for the rest of your life."

"Sweetheart, I am a hell of a lot faster than you are."

"We'll see."

"Be a good girl now and eat your eggs before I decide to take them away from you."

"*Bastard,*" she mumbled under her breath.

"Pardon me, princess?"

"This is good." Lifting her fork full of eggs, she shot him a nasty sneer.

Smirking, he picked up his toast and spoke. "I'll give you a few more Advil when you're done breakfast."

"I would appreciate that." They ate in silence for a few moments, enjoying the meal. "You make this?"

"No, I don't usually make a big breakfast. I'm more of a toast and coffee guy in the mornings. Quick and easy and I'm out the door."

"So, what is it you do for a living, besides kidnap innocent women?"

"I beat and torture small animals."

Her eyes lifted to his, scanning his body and shaking her head. "Obviously. And when you're not doing that, you…?"

She was fishing, he knew that. "Fly a space craft into outer space looking for other life forms."

"Ah, so they're still sending monkeys into space." She lifted her cup of coffee, her eyes lifting to meet his as she sipped.

He swallowed the food, thinking of a comeback that wouldn't end up backfiring on him, as they usually did. "Hey, even if I was a monkey, I sure as hell wouldn't be mooching off my father at the ripe old age of twenty eight."

Brilliant comeback. "I don't mooch." She snarled her response.

"You keep believing that, princess. Finished eating?"

"Yes."

Seeing that look in her eyes, he grabbed the fork from her hand before she could carry through with her threat.

Tucking it in his back pocket, out of her reach, he snatched the coffee cup from her fingers.

"Hey, give it back."

"Say bye-bye to the coffee, princess." Setting the mug on the tray with her plate, he scooped it up and set it near the door.

"You've got to be the rudest man I have ever met."

"Thank you." Taking her hand, biting his lip at the sneer on her face, he tied it back up to the post. "Don't have too much fun while I'm gone now."

"Jackass."

Laughing, he lifted the tray and left the room.

Chapter 15

With nothing but time on her hands, Liz watched the tree by the window as it danced in the wind. Tree—there was a tree outside the window. The bastard told her she would have had a long drop if she's managed to climb out the window. He lied to her. Well, duh, he is a kidnapper; it's not as if he'll tell you the truth.

Fuming, Liz watched the tree, through the damn bars no less, dancing in the wind. And she did not mooch off of her father. He gave her a monthly allowance—oh, God, how ridiculous did that sound. *Liz, dear God, you're twenty eight and you live off your father's money.* She was suddenly appalled.

She needed to do something with her life. What that something was, she just wasn't sure yet. Certainly not acting. She'd always detested acting, from childhood on. It had been the catalyst for every fight she and her father ever had.

She wondered how upset her father was by her absence. These past few years hadn't been very good to him. He'd been in a bit of a slump when it came to lucrative movie roles. Sure he'd had some offers, but he claimed they were beneath him, and he chose to wait for something better.

She was sure he and her mother had put up a good show for the cameras, letting the tears flow. Yet in the back of her mind, Liz couldn't help but wonder if they were a tiny bit relieved she was out of their hair. God knew she didn't always make it easy for them, with her rebellious jags and refusal to follow in his footsteps when it came to acting. And the rumors of her many love affairs—most of them false, but he hadn't believed her; he never believed in her.

It had never been her plan to follow in her father's footsteps. It wasn't her fault he hadn't had the son he'd hoped for, to mold in his image. And it wasn't her fault she had a stubborn streak to boot. Where did she get that from but her father? She blamed him for not understanding her better, for not accepting who she truly was.

Turning from the window, she sighed deeply. It didn't seem as though anyone was coming for her, so it was up to her to put an end to it. But how? She'd tried everything she could think of and yet she remained tied to the damn bed. She gave her arms a jerk, her shoulder singing with pain, reminding her of her injury.

What happened to the promise of giving her some Advil after breakfast? Insensitive jerk. Okay, that wasn't true; he wasn't insensitive to her, the exact opposite. And what kind of abductor treated his hostage with as much care as he did after her injury, and when she'd fainted. He even left her untied all night long. She regretted that she hadn't woken during the night. She might have been able to make a break for it then. Damn it.

Her mind drifted to the way her head felt against his chest and how gently he'd stroked her face. His hands were so soft against her cheek, caring when he rubbed her shoulder. His eyes, a dreamy pool of chocolate she could easily melt in and his lips... God, his lips looked so kissable, despite the limited view she had of them.

Get a grip, Liz, you need to get out of here, now. "Think, lunkhead, think, how could you break free?" She might be able to think more clearly if her head wasn't pounding. She paused, her mind working as the thought struck her. He left her untied all night long because she'd fallen and injured her head, which was probably the reason for her fainting spell in the bathroom. Bingo. All she needed to do is fake fainting and draw it out enough to make him worry about her and leave her untied...then what? Think, think.

Hearing the familiar sounds of footsteps coming towards her, she realized her time was up. Think later, act now. Letting her body go limp, she slumped forward, dropping her head and closing her eyes. Show time.

"Liz? Did you fall back asleep?"

She heard the door click shut, heard the floor creaking as he moved towards the bed. She didn't flinch a muscle.

"Liz? Liz? Oh shit."

Playing it to the fullest, she didn't move when he sat down in the bed beside her. When he laid a hand on her cheek, she nearly sighed with his gentleness.

"Come on, baby, talk to me."

Baby? Where did that come from? Her heart fluttered at the sentiment.

"Damn it, Liz, don't do this to me again." He began untying her hands. "I feel bad enough over this whole situation."

You should feel bad, buddy, she thought to herself, letting her body fall limply as he untied her.

"Come on, baby, please, open your eyes for me."

His hand stroked her face so softly she nearly buckled, but remained determined to carry this out, no matter what. She moaned, good and long, pretending to struggle to wake up.

"Liz, Liz, wake up now, okay? Come on." He continued patting her cheek.

"Wha...what happened?" She lifted her head, making it wobble.

"You blacked out again." Stroking her face, running his hand along the side of her head, he felt the lump. Parting her hair, he examined her head. "How do you feel?"

Right now she felt pretty damn comfortable in his arms while he stroked her hair and face. Letting out a deep breath, she plugged on. *Put your hormones aside, Liz, and stick to the plan.* "Terrible. My head is pounding." Which wasn't a complete lie.

"I'll get you some Advil and a bag of ice. That should help." He laid her on the bed, then walked to the door. Opening it, he called downstairs. "I need a bag of ice, could you bring it up to me?" He closed the door and hurried back to Liz.

"I could use a drink, if it isn't too much bother." Might as well make it good, Liz.

"Sure." He heard Terry heading up the stairs and met him at the door.

"What's up?"

"She's not doing so well. Can you pour her a glass of juice?"

"You're not calling it off, are you?"

"We'll see how she does." Taking the ice, he closed the door, and hurried to Liz. "Let's try this." He put the bag behind her head where the lump formed, plumping the pillow in the meantime.

"That feels nice."

"You've got a lump on your head from the fall; it's not open, which is good. I don't know what you were thinking."

I was thinking of getting the hell out of here, you imbecile. "I wasn't," she said instead, playing it to the fullest. Her eyes shifted as the door opened and Betty Rubble entered the room. Just the sight of the guy in that mask made her stomach curl.

"Thanks. I've got it from here." Taking the glass, Mac closed the door behind him, then turned to Liz. Setting the glass on the nightstand, he shook out two pills, then handed both pills and juice to her.

"Thank you." She took the glass and pills, making her hand shake as she lifted the glass to her lips. The tart orange juice touched her palate, shocking her.

"What you need is to rest, give the pills and the ice a chance to work."

"You're right." She held the glass out to him, indicating she finished with it, then slid back down onto the pillow when he took it. All she needed to do was wait, pretend to fall asleep and maybe he would leave her alone in the room. Then...well, then she would figure out how to make a break for it. There must be other windows in the house, other bedrooms she could sneak into. Closing her eyes, she lay still. Soon, very soon she would be free.

~

Leaving her to sleep, Mac walked to the nightstand and pulled out his book. He'd just sit and read while Liz slept. He didn't want to chance leaving her alone again, not until she felt better. The guilt over her illness and injury ate through his gut like acid.

Picking up his book, he began to read.

He felt the guilt slice into him. He hadn't meant to hurt her, but looking down at her lifeless body, he knew he'd done just that.

Mac snapped the book shut. Okay, so reading wasn't going to help. Setting the book down on the table, he let out a deep breath.

Damn, he felt like shit.

Chapter 16

She couldn't be sure how long she had slept, but Liz knew one thing for certain. The sun had gone down, engulfing her in complete darkness. She felt it choking her, grabbing hold of her lungs, squeezing tight, preventing the air from coming in or going out. Like a spider web, she felt trapped in the darkness, unable to move, to breathe, to do anything but quiver in fear.

Then, like a beacon in the night, the light pierced the darkness. A sliver of light shone through the crack of the opened door, and it felt like her salvation. She let out a rush of air and tried to calm down. Her heart pounded something fierce.

"Liz, are you awake?" Mac whispered as he stepped through the doorway.

Get a grip, Liz, pull it together, don't show your weakness. "Yes." She took a few deep breaths and thanked him silently for shedding some light into the room. He shut the door, the darkness grabbed hold and she nearly screamed out to bring the light back. When he clicked on the bedside lamp, she let out a silent cheer. She hated the darkness and she hated that it made her feel so weak.

"How do you feel?"

Better, now that there's light. "A little fuzzy. What time is it?"

"Nearly three." He set the tray on the bed.

"In the morning?" She couldn't see the clock to verify it, but by the darkness outside she accepted what he said to be true. Damn, he left her untied and alone, again, and she'd slept through it. Now what?

"Yeah, you've been asleep all day. How's your head?"

Time to continue the act. "I'm not sure, it's all so fuzzy. It's like there's a halo around everything." She rubbed her eyes.

"Let me take a look." He sat down beside her, helping her to sit. She started to sway, so he grabbed her by the arms. "Let's get you propped up." He tucked her against him while he pulled the pillows in behind her. "There you go, how is that?"

Oh, God, he felt so damn good holding her. "Better." *Stay in the moment.* She lifted her hand weakly and touched her fingers to her head. "I feel so woozy, like the bed's swaying beneath me."

"Maybe you're just weak from not eating all day. I brought up a sandwich, in case you woke up hungry."

She was starved, and the fact that he thought to bring her a sandwich touched something deep inside. "Thank you, a sandwich sounds nice."

Moving to the other side of the bed, he grabbed the plate holding the sandwich, carrying it back to her. "I hope you like ham."

His kindness and sweetness made her want to melt. *Stay with it, Liz, come on, girl.* "Ham is perfect." Making her hand shake again, she took the sandwich he held out to her and took a bite.

"You're awfully shaky. You've gone a long time without eating."

"Yeah." Feeling her bladder calling out for relief, Liz decided this might work to her advantage. "I need to use the washroom."

"Do you feel sick?" He set the plate down, prepared to help her if need be.

"Yeah, a little." She sat up, and he came right to her side to help her. *God, this is so hard.* It was supposed to be easy, yet he made her feel like crumbling in his arms.

"I've got you, princess." He held her up when her legs buckled. "Just lean on me, I've got you. I won't let anything happen to you."

Now that was dirty; the emotion in his voice struck a cord. *Push past it, Liz, and stay focused.* "The room is spinning…" She trailed off and let her full weight drop onto him, felt his strong arms scoop her up as he held her against him. *God, the power behind those arms was staggering, and the muscles in his chest were so— Stop it.*

"Everything's getting so fuzzy." She needed to stay in the moment, stick with the plan.

"Oh shit, princess, don't do this to me again. Come on."

He laid her back on the bed, patted her face with such gentleness and concern she felt the tears sting her eyes. No one had ever treated her with so much care. This man who held her hostage showed her more affection than her own parents ever had. It nearly broke her heart.

Giving her head a shake, she reminded herself of the reason for doing this. "Hmmm," she moaned.

"That's it. Come on, stay with me. Keep those pretty eyes focused on me now."

"I feel sick." She bolted up and stumbled to the door. She needed a moment alone, to gather her thoughts, to gather her strength. She slammed the bathroom door, then leaned against it, just trying to breathe.

"Do you need help?"

"No." She dropped down to the toilet, kneeling over the bowl, making it look good just in case he burst in. Sucking in a deep breathe, she made convincing gagging noises. Dipping her fingers into the toilet she imitated the sound of vomit splashing into the water. Oh, the price one must pay for freedom.

Mac took a few steps back; he needed distance before he hurled all over the carpet. What the hell was going on? He'd had enough, time to put an end to it all. Rushing to the door, he thrust it open, and called for the phone.

Bolting up the stairs, Terry handed Mac the phone. "What's going on? Is she okay?"

"No. I'm calling him. I don't like this; I think she's got a concussion." Taking the phone, Mac leaned against the door as he dialed the number, his hand shaking.

"*Hello.*"

"There's a problem," Mac blurted out the instant the call was answered.

"*Oh?*"

"It's Liz, she's sick." Mac ran a hand through his hair, catching the mask. Frustrated, he slipped it back in place.

"*Is that all?*"

Mac's hand tensed on the phone, knuckles turning white as bone. "Listen, Cromwell, it's serious, I think she needs a doctor. She's vomiting and she's blacked out a few times now. What's a few more days, anyway?" Cromwell was slime for doing this, and he was slime for going along with it.

"*Plenty. Elizabeth has always been overly dramatic. She'll be fine, there are only a few more days left.*"

"Look Cromwell—"

"*No, you look, Mr. Tyrell, I am in charge here; you do as I say or I will go to the police and tell them you've been blackmailing me.*"

Mac's face lit with fury. "Then I'll just have to set them straight."

"*Please, Mr. Tyrell, who do you think the police will believe?*"

Mac knew damn well who they would believe. And he didn't have any proof to back up his side of the story. No way would the cops believe him over one of the most famous, wealthy men on the planet. "Fine, what do you suggest I do to help your daughter in the mean time?"

"*Give her some anti-nausea medication and plenty of rest, I suppose. I can't be bothered with this now.*"

Mac wished he could slide his hands through the telephone and wring the old guy's neck. *Can't be bothered, she's your fucking daughter, you slimy bastard.* "I don't have anything in the house for that."

"*Then get some, send Orsini.*"

"He could be spotted."

"*You wore masks, correct?*"

"Yes," Mac snarled into the phone.

"*And you used the unregistered van?*"

Mac's eyes slanted. "Yes."

Kidnapped

"Then what is the problem? Use another vehicle and get it done. Now stop bothering me."

Mac disconnected the call and swore. He wanted so badly to throw the phone across the room.

"Not good, I take it?"

"The guy is a selfish, uncaring bastard." And that was putting it mildly. Why did he only now realize that?

"That's the consensus among most people. What did he say?"

Mac handed Terry the phone before he smashed it against the wall. "To deal with her." His eyes lifted to Terry. "Take my car and run into the city and grab something for nausea." He shook his head. "He wasn't even the slightest bit concerned for his own daughter's well being."

"And that surprises you?"

Looking at it all now, a father wanting his own child kidnapped for fame, did it get any worse than that? "Take the cell phone, Terry, in case there's a problem."

"Okay, I'll get going."

~

Liz closed the bathroom door, turned the water on in the sink and cursed. Anger gripping her, she grabbed hold of the sides of the sink, lowering her head. *That lowdown, uncaring, selfish bastard.* He's the one in charge, he arranged for her to be kidnapped. Her father had been the one.

The tears spilled out from her eyes and dropped into the sink to blend in with the running water. How could he do this to her? What had she done to warrant such a cruel punishment? She was sure she was being punished for something she'd done.

"Liz?"

She jumped at the knock. Looking up into the mirror, she nearly gasped at how awful she looked. Her eyes looked red and swollen and her face pale and drenched with tears. "Yeah." She closed her eyes, took a deep breath, then wiped the tears from her face and straightened.

She knew when she opened the door, he would be waiting for her as usual. The emotions racing through her right now were so strong, she thought she might explode. But she needed to remain calm, think, plan.

"Are you okay?"

"I've been better." No truer words were ever said.

"Need a hand?"

She wiped her face once more, figured the blood shot eyes would play nicely, and stepped from the bathroom. "I believe I do, thank you."

She heard the roar of an engine, then gravel spitting, and figured the other guy had left. Perfect. "Could I bother you for some more juice?" She nearly crumbled when he ran his hand over her hair.

"Sure."

Her lips quivered with a smile as she lay down on the bed, his hands leaving an unsettling sensation on her head.

"I'll be right back." He left her on the bed and rushed from the room.

Liz sat up, glanced around the room for something to use to knock him out, and spotted the wrought iron lamp on the night stand. Pity, it was such a nice lamp. Lifting it, surprised at its weight but glad for it, she walked to the door and waited for him to return. This time, she would win.

"You're going down, big guy," she whispered, hearing him rushing up the steps. Like a spider spinning its web, she waited for her prey. When he stepped through the door, she lifted the lamp, then sent it crashing down over his head.

Like it all happened in slow motion, she watched as he tumbled to the floor, his large frame thudding as he hit bottom. The glass in his hand splashed to the floor, orange juice soaking into the cream toned carpet. She looked down as Bart crumbled at her feet.

Chapter 17

Jumping up with a squeal of joy, Liz stared down at his slumped body on the floor, out cold.

"Take that." Dropping the lamp, she jumped over his body, then ran down the long flight of stairs and towards freedom. She was free now, and God help her father when she caught up to him. She ran for the back door and stopped cold when she saw the complete darkness outside. As if a blanket had been draped over the world, the darkness surrounded her. There wasn't a light to be seen.

"Come on, Liz, this is your chance, don't blow it now." She sucked in a deep breath, then turned to look for keys. One of these sets hanging on the wall must belong to that retched van they'd used to kidnap her, but which one?

So it had been her father who arranged for her to be taken. She wiped the single tear that slipped from her eyes. Could it be from the betrayal of her father, or because she'd fallen for the man who helped? She ran a hand through her long, tussled hair, mindful of the bump, and thought as she scanned the row of keys before her. What did they say about a woman scorned? Thinking, she walked back into the kitchen.

If she ran now, if she got away and told the police of her ordeal, what would happen? If she was lucky, they would go to the house and find the big guy still unconscious. But what about her father? Would they believe her when she told them that her father set it all up? She didn't think so. Her father was too smart, he'd find a way out of it.

What she needed was answers. Seeing the telephone on the table, her mind working, she picked it up, tapping it in her palm. The only person she felt that might give her a decent answer would be her abductor. And if she played her cards right, he would be singing like a canary. That is, if she could manage to do what needed to be done. Sucking in a deep breath, she ran up the stairs, finding him still on the floor, in the exact spot he'd fallen, the lamp to his left, the spilled glass to his right. It was perfect. Setting the telephone on the nightstand, she went to him.

"It's payback time, and you know what they say about it being a bitch." Sliding her arms under his, she lifted him, cursing when her shoulder cried out in pain.

"Damn, you're heavy." She shifted him, bit back the pain and hoped he didn't wake up. "Must be all that muscle." Grunting, she dragged him to the bed. Taking a moment to catch her breath, she wiped her brow, then stepped onto the bed.

"God, I hope I can do this." Leaning down, she hooked her arms under his, took in a few deep breaths, then lifted. "Holy crap." It certainly wasn't easy; his weight sent pain into her shoulder. Biting back the burning pain not only from her shoulder, but her abs and arms as well, she carried on. The man definitely had a lot to him.

He fell on her, she grunted, he moaned, she hustled. Sliding out from under him, she shifted him on the bed. "Okay, big guy, it's my turn to play bondage."

Lifting his arms, she tied each wrist to the post, good and tight. "That should do it." Climbing from the bed, she wiped the sweat from her brow and caught her breath.

"Okay, let's have a look under this ridiculous mask." Her fingers paused only for a moment before she slid the mask from his face. She gasped, the silly cartoon mask slipping from her fingers to fall on the carpeted floor. "Oh, God, you're handsome." She sat down on the edge of the bed and took a good long look at the man that had held her captive for several days.

His face was tanned and rugged with heavy cheek bones and a cleft in his chin. And those lips, full and tempting, that spouted off to her so many times, tempting her mouth. His dark curly hair caressed the collar of his shirt.

"Now why couldn't you have been hideous? It would make this so much easier." She let out a long sigh, then stood.

Lifting the glass off the floor, she walked to the bathroom and ran the water good and cold before filling the glass. Taking a moment just to admire the beauty of the man that lay in the bed, she let out a sigh, then sent the cold water plummeting to his face.

His eyes flew open wide, he sputtered, tried to put a hand to his face, and couldn't.

"Hello there." Liz stood over him with a devious smile.

"Liz?" He tried to sit up and couldn't, his tied hands prevent him. "What the hell is going on?"

"A little poetic justice. Don't bother struggling. Like you, I'm quite good at tying knots." The pride rang in her voice as she stood over him.

"Untie me, Elizabeth." He jerked his arms, tugging to break free.

She laughed, not a quick frivolous laugh, but one filled with humor at the situation. "Oh, this is too much fun."

"Oh, yeah, real funny. Now untie me," he demanded.

Her face grew sober as she leaned in over him. "I'm in charge now, big guy, and I'll untie you when I'm damn good and ready." Looking down into that gorgeous face, his eyes staring up at her, she felt a pang of guilt. The memory of how he'd looked at her when he'd thought she'd been ill struck her suddenly and made her heart ache. *Stay strong*, she reminded herself, then spotting the cloth he'd used on her face earlier, she found her solution. It would be so much easier to get to the truth if she didn't have to look into his kind eyes.

For a second he wasn't sure what she was going to do with the cloth. Shoving it in his mouth came to mind. But then she laid it over his eyes, her fingers brushing his cheek, then slipping through his hair to tie the cloth at the back of his head. "What are you doing that for?" He felt her hair caress his cheek, her breath on his face, sending a ripple of desire through his body, and for a brief second he wanted nothing more than to have her take him here and now.

"I think you need to see how it feels to be in the dark. What's your name?" When he didn't answer, she demanded just a bit stronger. "Name."

"Mac." He felt rather unsettled, not knowing what she was doing. He could tell she moved around the room by the way her voice carried, and if he was right, she stood near the foot of the bed. He felt his loins tightening and his gut clench. The mixture of lust and fear was an odd sensation.

"Mac, I like it. You're going to make a call, Mac."

"Am I now? That's a little hard to do when I'm blindfolded and tied to the fucking bed!" He emphasized the last a little louder.

"Grumpy, aren't we? Not to worry, Mac, I'll dial and hold it to your ear."

"Grumpy, I am beyond fucking grumpy. Now untie me."

She clucked her tongue in a way a mother would to a disobedient child. "Now, Mac, no need to get upset. If you're a good boy, I might even give you a candy."

"You are pushing it, lady," he warned her, trying to gauge where she stood in the room. He could smell her familiar light scent and while it aroused his senses, not knowing what she was doing pissed him off.

"Oh, Mac, you don't frighten me. Even if you weren't tied to the bed, you wouldn't frighten me. Now, let's make that call, shall we?"

Mac snarled, gritting his teeth. "Who the hell am I calling?

"Betty Rubble, what's the cell number?"

Blind to her movements, he found himself stimulated, imaging what she might be doing. He could picture her perfectly in his mind, the way she moved her body, her hips swaying ever so gently as she walked, her head held high, her long golden hair falling just short of her breasts…

"What's the number Mac?"

"I have no idea," he snapped back.. When she sat down beside him, his body tensed up. The touch of her hand on his face startled him, drawing out both lust and worry.

"Didn't your mother ever tell you it isn't nice to lie? I heard you tell him to take the cell in case there was a problem. Now, what's the number?"

Clenching his jaw, Mac recited the number.

"Good, now, you are going to tell him that I got worse, you called my father and he told you to take me home, and that he'll be in touch with him later."

The phone touched his ear but it was the feel of her fingers on his skin that he felt the most. He imagined quite vividly how they would feel running along his chest, cupping hold of his—he snapped out of his lustful fantasy when the phone was answered. "Terry, its Mac. Don't bother coming back here."

"What? Why?"

"She's getting worse. I called Cromwell and he said to bring her home."

"Home, shit. Did he mention when I would be getting the movie role?"

"He'll be in touch."

"Say good bye, Mac," Liz whispered against his ear, making him shiver.

"Gotta go."

"Good boy, Mac. Well done. And as a reward, I'll remove this." With one simple tug, the blindfold slid away.

"You were faking the whole time?" he asked with disdain, blinking his eyes as they attempted to readjust to the light.

A smile lighting her eyes, Liz commented with pride, "You bet. Fooled you big time, didn't I?"

"I should have known better."

"Don't feel too bad, Mac, I've fooled many people. You weren't the first." She patted his leg and smiled when he snarled. "Now, I want the story. Start from the beginning and don't leave anything out." She pulled the pack of cigarettes from his breast pocket, and lit one up. "Oh, God, that's great, I've been dying for one for days." She blew the smoke out in tiny little rings, then waved her hand for him to continue. "Do begin."

Clenching his jaw, he began. "Your father approached me three months ago. At first I thought he'd mistaken me for someone else, because he'd never given me the time of day before. He started talking; saying how he heard I was in a bind and that I would benefit from his plan. I shrugged, he began to talk. He planned to have me kidnap you. I would hold you here, at my farm for one week, then release you."

"Why?"

"Why what?"

She blew a heavy cloud of smoke in his face and snarled. "Why did he do it?"

Mac let out a heavy sigh. "Publicity."

"Publicity?"

"Yes, he figured he would get plenty of it with you being kidnapped, the press would be on him and it would in turn boost his career."

"How do you know my father?"

Mac blinked in utter shock. "Uh, I've done some stunt work on a few of his movies."

"You're a stunt man?"

"Yes."

"Well, I guess that's why the chair didn't have much effect on you." She drew on the cigarette, then crushed it out in three swift easy movements. "You'd be used to such things."

"Although it's been years since a chair's been broken over my back, I recall them using a prop, not the real deal." He paused, giving her a heated look. "I assure you, I was affected."

She shrugged her shoulders carelessly. "I guess I should have used the lamp in the first place, it was more effective."

"Because you could lift it higher, heave it down harder," he informed her through gritted teeth.

"Apparently." She smiled.

"I was only doing my job Liz."

"Doing your job? Let's discuss that job, shall we, Mac? Did my father tell you to tie me up?"

"Yes."

"And the other guy, Terry, did my father tell him to rough me up, to…"

"Liz, I'm sorry that happened. I didn't want him involved."

"Then why was he?"

"He's the son of a friend of your father's."

"And the two of you had no problem doing this to me. Why you, what are you getting from this?"

He drew in a deep breath. "I did it because the money was too tempting to turn down, and I knew you would be in good hands."

"Money, let us discuss that." She leaned forward, tapped her fingers on her knee. "How much were you getting paid?"

He paused. "Two hundred thousand."

She let out a snort. "Oh, God, Mac, that's chump change to my father. He pays his gardener more than that a year. Oh, Mac, you got hosed."

He didn't take kindly to her laughter. "Two hundred thousand may not be much to you, Liz, but it goes a long way for a guy like me who needed it to keep the only home he has ever known. Now, joke's over, you can untie me."

"Not yet. Tell me what you mean by needing the money to keep your home."

"My father died a year ago, in debt. I didn't know that

until his funeral. He'd been close to losing this farm and needed fifty thousand to save it from being foreclosed. This is the only home I've have ever had; there was no damn way I was letting it go. So I agreed to your father's...idea."

"Why didn't you just get a loan from the bank?"

"I tried, but no one would touch me. Your father approached me at just the right time."

She stood suddenly. "I need to take a walk."

"I'm still tied up, are you just going to leave me here?" He jerked his hands, indicating she'd yet to untie him.

She smiled now, sweetly. "Oh yes, I think I will, for just a bit longer. I need the key, though, to lock you in here before I leave."

He smirked. "Search for it."

"I don't have to; I know exactly where it is." Her hand paused briefly over his left pocket before she slid her fingers inside.

Everything inside of him that was male came to attention. Despite the situation, having her hand that close to his vital organ could not be ignored.

"Is that a key in your pocket, Mac, or are you just happy to see me?" She pulled the key out and held it up, dangling it from her finger, a mocking grin on her face. "I suppose that would be considered an insult to your manhood, since the key isn't very big

"You're a laugh riot, Liz. I'm splitting a gut here."

Biting her lip, smirking, Liz turned to the door. "Get comfy, Mac, you might be there a while."

Mac heard the door click, then the lock engaged and he blew out a long breath of air. There had to be something seriously wrong with him to be feeling turned on by all this bondage. Because in the end, he feared he wouldn't get out of it what he truly needed.

Chapter 18

Being cooped up for so long, Liz headed outside first. The sun was just beginning to rise; its brilliant hues of red and orange filling the sky touched something deep within her. With her father's fame, her face being recognized due to his public displays of her as a child and youth, she found it hard to just venture outdoors often. So much of her life had been wasted inside, locked away from everything.

Breathing in the cool crisp dawn air, Liz took a moment to just enjoy. There was land as far as the eye could see, and not another house in the area. Trees lined the property, filling in empty space. Not crowding, but adding to the beauty of the land. Grass, full lush green grass ran endlessly in all directions, immaculately kept. There were flowers, tiny baby's breath surrounding tall gloriously bright lilies in barrels at each corner of the patio. Rose bushes stood regally protecting the barrier of the home, and wooden benches sat in an angle so that one could admire the beauty before them. This was a home. Nothing compared to the cold sterile mansion she'd grown up in.

There was pride here, love for one's property.

He'd needed the money to save this place.

Okay, so it wasn't the smartest way to get money, but he'd had a real reason for wanting the money. This was a gorgeous place after all, and his family home. Would she have done something as drastic as kidnap someone for money to save her family home? No, because family didn't mean that much to her, not, as it obviously did, to Mac. She had no sentiment for her home; it could burn to the ground for all she cared. There were no fond memories, but for Mac, she could understand how this home would have plenty. Enough for him to risk it all and take a woman captive to get a measly two hundred thousand bucks.

Two hundred thousand dollars, how humiliating. Her

father could afford more than that, and what did it say about her worth in his eyes? Mac's comment about the banks not loaning him the money made her think that possibly her father persuaded them not to give Mac the loan. She wouldn't put it past her father.

Sitting down on the wooden bench, she let out a heavy sigh. She'd been brought to this place, held against her will, and never allowed to see, to partake in the beauty, to enjoy the freedom. Wasn't that her life in a nut shell?

You must show dignity, Elizabeth, never step from the house unless dressed suitably, always hold your head high and never embarrass the Cromwell name.

Her father's words buzzed in her head like an annoying bee ready to sting. She'd obeyed him as a child, but as she'd matured into an adult, she found she had enough of being his puppet.

That's when she began to rebel, and the paparazzi captured every sordid detail. Caught drunk and disorderly, damn her father for paying off the judge. She'd been video taped at a late night party house, draped over a man in a heated embrace. She had a slew of speeding tickets, smashed a few cars, and had generally caused enough mayhem to give her father major stress. And she'd gotten the attention she'd craved.

Look, Daddy, pay attention to me, see *me*. But in time she came to realize the attention she acquired had been the wrong kind. Yes, her father tried to keep a closer eye on her, but not by being with her. He just hired more guards and restricted her privacy, her money and cars. And the tabloids labeled her *The Angel from Hell*. Reports stated that she'd been addicted to drugs, alcohol and pain killers. They spouted that she'd been unstable and ready to crack. They didn't know how close to the truth they'd been.

She detested the paparazzi, she despised notoriety, and she hated her father. *Yes, Elizabeth, admit it for once, you hate your father.*

Her father pushed her all of her life to follow in his

footsteps towards an acting career. And she'd had no desire to do so. He'd pushed her towards a modeling career, she purposely gained twenty pounds. He wanted to mold her to his liking, and he never gave a damn about what she wanted. And once again he did what was best for him and ignored her feelings.

How demented was her father to hire two men to kidnap her, hold her captive, all for his fame? *Well, Daddy, this time you will see who your precious little girl really is, and you will see that I am no push over. I won't stand for being treated no better than a dog you train and kick aside when you no longer have use for it. This time, you've gone too far.*

She sat alone in the light of the early dawn morning, reflecting.

~

Well, isn't this just fucking perfect, Mac thought bitterly as he gave his arms a solid tug. *Who would have thought the woman a pro at tying knots? Well, the tables certainly have been turned, now haven't they, Mac?* Frowning, he looked towards the window. He deserved it, though, didn't he? And really, he should be glad she'd tied him to the bed and not to the chair he'd kept her in most of the time. Aside from tying him to his own bed, she really was treating him kindly.

Why?

He deserved to be treated like crap for what he'd done to her. She should be furious. He would be if his father did to him what Cromwell had done to his child. *What a bastard. And what does that make you, Mac? You participated in his sick plot to gain fame. Sure, you can justify it by saying you needed the money. But...*

Letting out a deep breath, he stared up at the ceiling. Could use a coat of paint. Then again, what's the point, he thought. He was going to lose it all when Liz went to the cops and turned him in. Closing his eyes, he waited. What else could he do?

Liz wiped her face dry and lit up a cigarette. Mac's tastes were a bit stronger than she preferred, but it served its purpose. She drew in long and deep, letting the strong sting of tobacco fill her mouth before she blew out a dozen smoke rings that lingered in the still air. She pictured each ring wrapped around her father's neck until he choked, pleading to her for air. She smiled, took another drag.

What was her mother's role in this whole attempt at regaining fame, she wondered bitterly? Did she even know what her husband had been up to? Doubtful. Eliza Cromwell's head was too far stuck up her socialite ass to even notice her daughter missing. And even if she noticed, she probably sat wringing her hands, putting on a good show for the cameras.

She might not be acting any longer, but her mother never refused an opportunity to play the wounded damsel. Was it any wonder she and her father made such a perfect pair? They were both of the same stock.

Her hand unsteady as she lifted the cigarette to her lips, Liz drew in, fuming. Well, the time had come for a plan. She wanted revenge. Her father needed to pay, and she wanted him to pay dearly. She would ruin him, ruin his precious career. See who gets the last laugh now, Daddy dearest. She watched as a set of blue jays fought over territory on a small tree limb.

What would the tabloids say when she called them with an exclusive and explained to them what had happened to her and who'd instigated it?

She realized suddenly she couldn't do that to Mac. Yes, he kidnapped her, held her against her will, tied her up, but he'd treated her kindly. If it hadn't been for him, the slimy bastard...what was his name again?...Terry, yes, Terry would have had his way with her. She shuddered with the memory, feeling his hands on her still. Mac saved her from Terry, protected her from the bastard and had even been kind to her. And Mac had been incredibly caring to her when her attempt to beak free caused her to fall and hit her head. The way he'd pleaded for her to wake up when he thought she was truly ill. The way his hand had stroked her face, her hair, so gently, was staggering.

She couldn't send him to jail. He had, after all, been used by her father as well. She still had time, she hoped, before her father would expect the whole ordeal to end. She knew she wouldn't be able to keep Mac tied up the entire time, just long enough for him to agree to her plan. She just needed to come up with a plan that was too good for him to resist.

Taking a long drag from her cigarette, Liz thought of ways to make her father pay. What did he value more than anything else in his life? It wasn't her, he made that brutally clear. It wasn't just money, though he did value it, but something else, his reason for this whole fiasco. *Oh, you made a vital mistake, Daddy. You miscalculated your daughter's capabilities*, she thought bitterly. After all, it had been he who'd taught her to set her sights high and never stop until you got what you wanted. And oh, how she wanted this.

Sliding from the bench, she tapped the cigarette out in a flower pot. Unable to resist, she picked a few roses from the bush and a few lilies from the flower beds and drew in their scent. What she wanted now was a nice hot shower. A change of clothing would be nice but that could wait. Taking the fresh cut flowers into the house, she decided to have a look around before her shower.

Payback was a bitch and her name is Elizabeth Cromwell.

Chapter 19

To Mac's calculations, Liz had been gone well over two hours. He would be able to tell the time from his watch if his goddamn hands weren't tied to the bed. The clock that usually sat on his nightstand had been shifted, most likely when Liz grabbed the lamp. His head was itchy, and he couldn't do anything but lay here letting it drive him nuts. And he wanted a goddamn cigarette.

Okay, so his mood was sour. He was hungry, sore, his head hurt, and the guilt over what he participated in was eating him up alive. Mac had no idea what Liz's plans might be for him, but whatever they were, he deserved it. *You're a louse, Mac, for thinking of money over the well being of an innocent person. Idiot.* Man, how quickly his life had turned upside down.

And to top it off, he felt something more for the damn prima donna. It wasn't just lust. He'd realized that when she'd become ill, or faked her illness rather. Okay, so that pissed him off. He'd been genuine in his worry for her, and she'd played him. Damn it. He was a fly caught in her spider's web and to top it off, he was pretty damn sure he was in love with her.

He must have lost his mind. First agreeing to kidnap an innocent person for money to save his home, then falling for the very woman he'd been hired to hold for a week. Liz was probably going to send him to jail as well. *Damn stupid idiot, Mac. Serves you right.*

He heard her footsteps heading towards him and thought, *this is it*. Letting out a long breath, he waited for his punishment.

~

Setting the donut on top of the glass, Liz unlocked the door. She felt so much better after her shower. The moment she stepped into the room, Mac's head turned to her and their eyes met. She didn't see anger this time, but something different. His eyes looked softer, like they'd been when she'd been injured. Shaking it off, she moved into the room. "Did you miss me Mac?"

"Oh, yeah, about as much as I miss dental drills."

"Aren't they irritating?" She moved into the room.

"Nearly as irritating as being tied to this bed." He jerked his hands.

"Yes, I can attest to that, and you are right, it is irritating." Smirking, she walked to the plush chair Mac had slept in the first night and took a seat. Now why couldn't he have tied her to this chair instead of the damn hard one?

"Untie me, Liz."

"Now, Mac, you're forgetting who is in charge here."

"Okay, I get that you're pissed but—"

"Pissed? Pissed? I am way beyond pissed, Mac. But not to worry, most of my anger is aimed towards my father."

"Lucky me, yet I'm the one tied to the bed," he grumbled, giving his arms a tug to emphasize his point.

"You're grumpy, probably from lack of food. Here, have a bite." She shoved the sugar glazed donut in his mouth, nearly to the half way point before she pulled it away. "I tied you up so I could think." She lifted the wine to her lips and sipped. "God, I missed this. Would it have killed you to have shared your stock with me?" She shrugged it off when she saw his mouth full. "In any case, it's my turn to cause you grief now, Mac." She set her wine glass on the nightstand.

He swallowed the donut and laughed. "*Princess*, you've done nothing but cause me grief."

She shoved the rest of the donut in his mouth, then licked her fingers clean. "How many times do I have to tell you to quit calling me that?" She pulled out a cigarette, ran it through her fingers.

He swallowed and just couldn't resist. "Ten, no wait, twelve." He snickered.

The lighter clicked on to light up a less than impressed

face. "For someone who is tied to a bed, you sure are fucking witty." She took a good hard drag from her cigarette, her eyes focused on him.

"You know, I thought the very same thing about you. You never took me seriously."

"In the beginning I did, I was terrified, but the more I was around you, the more I realized you weren't the one to be afraid of."

"Maybe I should have picked a demon mask; I might have gotten some respect from you."

"Oh, Mac, don't you know, it had nothing to do with that silly mask." She waved her cigarette towards the mask on the floor, smoke floating in circles. "You just don't frighten me. You're eyes are too kind."

"Well, then, maybe I should have worn red contacts. You know, those ones they have now that look like cat's eyes or flames." The corner of his mouth turned up in a faint smirk.

She smiled slyly. "You know, Mac, given normal circumstances, I think we might have hit it off."

"I doubt if you would have even given me a second look prin—Liz." He corrected when her eye brow shot up.

She leaned back and enjoyed her wine and cigarette. "Why is that, Mac?"

"I'm not a playboy millionaire or some model off the runway."

She took her time sipping from her glass. "Why am I not surprised that you believe that trash. So you think you have me pegged, huh, Mac?"

"Pretty much, yeah."

"Well, congratulations, Mac, you are one of the many millions who seem to think they know me so well." She leaned in real close and blew the smoke down into his face. "But you don't know dick."

"Okay, Liz, why don't you enlighten me and tell me who you are?"

She leaned back because she was too damn tempted to

kiss him. "Perhaps another time. For now, I need some answers." She lifted her wine to ease the craving for his lips.

"Well, isn't that a pity, I left all my answers in my other pants." He shot her a bright smile.

"See, now that's why I think we would get along. We both have a wicked sense of humor." She leaned in, placed her cigarette between his lips and let him have a drag. "Do you check in with my father on a daily basis?" She leaned back, crushed the cigarette out in the ashtray and waited.

"No."

She lifted her wine glass, swirling the contents. "When is the next time you're to contact him?" She put the glass to her lips, drank and let the spicy wine settle on her tongue before she swallowed. He had excellent taste in wine. *Bravo to you, Mac.*

"I don't contact him unless there's a problem."

She remembered the call earlier. "Will Terry contact my father if he doesn't hear from him soon?"

He shrugged. "I haven't a clue."

"Well, let's make sure. I wouldn't want him spoiling all my fun." Smiling deviously, Liz stood to grab the phone that sat on the bed. "Guess I forgot to move this, bad me." She put a hand to her lips and giggled. "Not that you were up to making a call, that is."

Laughing, she walked to the chair again and sat. "Okay, Mac, here's what you're going to say. Tell Terry that my father insisted he lay low, stay in hiding for a few days. Tell him that I'm home and that my father intends to play it out the full time, then he'll be in contact." Liz held her hand over the digits. "Understood?"

"Yes, boss."

"See, you replied with sarcasm. I so love being sarcastic." Laughing, she pressed send, then laid the phone against his ear and listened while he explained everything in detail to Terry. She could smell his scent and it stirred a longing inside of her to snuggle up beside him. She shook her head clear when he finished speaking. Setting the phone down on the nightstand, she continued. "I don't know what relationship you have with Terry, but he isn't a very nice guy."

"I can't stand the guy. Look, about his behavior—"

"Let's not go there, okay?" She sat back in the chair, swinging her foot restlessly. "What was his motivation for this job?"

Accepting that she didn't want to discuss Terry, he let it go. "An acting role in your father's next big movie."

Her brow creased. "What big movie?" He didn't have any big movie.

"The big movie your abduction and publicity would provide him."

Nodding, Liz understood. "So he's an actor. Remind me never to watch anything he's in. Okay, Terry did it for a movie role, you did it for money to save your farm and my father arranged it for publicity." She stood now, anger making her restless. "And did anyone think what this ordeal would do to me?"

"Liz—"

"My father was so busy wanting what he'd lost that he didn't give a damn about my feelings." She snorted. "Like that's anything new to me." Though it still hurt.

"I didn't think it out hard enough. If I had—"

"When I was seven, I was in the hospital having my appendix removed. Did you know that neither of my parents were there when I woke up, or to hold my hand before surgery? I received a bouquet of yellow roses and a teddy bear. That's it. My nanny came to take me home while my parents attended a dinner party."

"Liz—"

"This is just one more example of how much my father cares for me." The tears stung her eyes. "He uses whatever he can, whomever he can, to get what he wants and doesn't give a damn who he steps on as he makes his way to the top."

"I'm sorry, Liz, I am truly sorry."

Catching herself, Liz sniffled back her tears, slipped her hand into her pocket and pulled out the key. She didn't say a word as she ran from the room, her feet barreling on the wooden steps.

Grabbing a kitchen chair, she plopped down and, her eyes blurry with hot tears, she wept. All of her life she'd wanted only one thing from her parents, mainly her father, and that was love. Yet neither gave it to her. She'd been in denial apparently, thinking he cared at least a tiny bit for her. This ordeal showed her he didn't. Had he ever?

Wiping the tears from her cheeks, Liz sat back, her eyes glancing around the room. The early morning sun lit the kitchen, brightening it, while the light breeze floated through the thin lace curtains making them dance.

The counter looked worn, as if it had been through many years of use. All the appliances were in white, as were the cupboards. Painted a deep green, the walls were a stark contrast against the white in the room. Everything was spotless.

This was Mac's home. He'd taken her to his home. Taking one of the lilies from his flower beds, she sniffed it, her mind wandering to the man tied to the bed upstairs.

He was an incredibly handsome, rugged, witty man. He had kindness in him, there were times she saw a hint of temper, yet he'd never raised a hand to her. She knew virtually nothing about him, yet her heart yearned to have him.

It wasn't Stockholm Syndrome, she really did have feelings for him. She hadn't seen his face, or even known who he was, yet she'd felt something for him.

She couldn't explain it, but she knew that being near him made her feel like she'd never felt before. Sure he irritated her, but that was the fun of it.

Sighing, Liz dropped her head on the table, cursing herself for her stupidity when she was reminded of the lump on her head. What did it matter if she felt something for Mac? He didn't feel the same for her. Why would he? She was nothing more than a job to him. Wishing desperately that he could love her, Liz lifted her head.

What she needed now was to cook. She always cooked when she was upset. Pushing from the chair, which she noticed matched the one she'd been tied to in the bedroom, Liz went to the fridge. While she pulled out ingredients, she hoped Mac would go along with her plan. What would she do if he didn't?

Money. He needed it, she—well, her father— certainly had plenty of it. No one could refuse money. Money was much easier to accept than…love.

Sighing, Liz began chopping vegetables.

Chapter 20

Carrying the overfilled tray up the stairs was no easy feat. It was a task just trying to keep the glasses from tumbling over, and a chore to keep the tray from tipping as she moved up the stairs. By the time she reached the bedroom door, Liz gained a new respect for waitresses. Setting the tray on the floor, she noticed not a drop of wine had spilled and smiled; it wasn't so hard after all. She pulled the key from her pants pocket and disengaged the lock. Opening the door, bending to lift the tray, she stepped into the room and found Mac sound asleep.

The heaviness of the tray forgotten, she stood and just watched him sleep. God, he was easy on the eyes, she mused. Not playboy handsome, not runway handsome, just striking. Rugged.

It hadn't been his face that stirred her, since he'd kept that hidden from her the whole time. She wasn't quite sure what drew her in; all she knew was that he did something to her heart.

When he stirred, she realized she still stood by the door with the heavy tray in her hands. Setting it on the chair, she walked to the bed. Her first thought was to lie down beside him and wake him with a long lazy kiss, but she dismissed that quickly enough. In time, after he got to know who she truly was, maybe. So she gave him a hard shove instead. "Rise and shine, Mac, lunch is ready."

He grumbled something in the line of wanting her dead. She smiled and gave him another shove. "Come on, big guy, I made us lunch."

"Now that's a pleasant sight to wake up to."

She stood locked to her spot, unable to move after such a comment. When her mind managed to click back into gear, she shook it off and turned away. Whoa, that hit her heart with a mighty blow. "I hope you like this, it's one of my specialties." She lifted the tray and turned to the bed. "I was grateful that you had all the ingredients in the house." She set the tray on the bed.

He took in the aromatic scent and sighed. "You can cook?"

"Of course I can cook."

"Real food, not microwavable dinners?"

Her eyes narrowed, her hands came up to her hips and she spoke with deep sarcasm. "Though it was a task for me to figure out how to turn the oven on and mix a few things together, I managed. But you might want to consider putting some of that money you'll be receiving from my father towards fixing the scorch marks on the kitchen wall." She giggled nervously. "I accidentally lit it on fire."

"What?" Mac bolted forward, apparently forgetting he was bound to the bed.

Laughing, Liz walked to the side of the bed. "I'm joking, Mac. I can cook, and cook quite well."

"My kitchen is still intact?"

She smirked. "Yes, Mac."

"Thank God. That wasn't funny."

"Really? I thought it was. You should have seen the look on your face. Priceless. I have a proposition for you, Mac, that I think you are going to like. If I untie one hand, do you promise to give me a chance before trying to kill me?"

"If I wanted to kill you Liz, I would have done it long ago." He gave her a wide, devious smile.

"You're a pussy cat, Mac, you couldn't hurt anyone. Now, can I trust you? Or do I feed you this wonderful meal I slaved over?"

"I'll behave." When she tilted her head, he amended. "I promise I'll behave and give you a chance. Now hand that food over already, I'm starved."

She hoped she wasn't making a mistake by untying one hand. As her fingers caressed his wrist, untying the knots, she felt his pulse speed up. She wasn't sure what to think of that, so she stepped back after releasing the last knot. "Here you go."

Kidnapped

He sat up, taking the plate. "Smells good."

"Thank you, vegetarian stir fry à la Liz." She gave a mock bow and beamed.

He stabbed one of the vegetables and slipped it into his mouth.

She caught the surprise in his eyes. "It's spicy, I prefer things hot, livens up the taste buds, challenges the palate." She handed him his glass of wine. "Masks the taste of the poison I slipped into the food." She burst out laughing as the food in his mouth went flying onto his plate. "Oh, Mac, Mac, Mac. I was kidding. Don't be scared, you should know my humor by now."

"Your humor *is* what scares me." He hesitated, his fork hovering over his plate.

"Oh, for heavens sake." Stabbing a carrot slice on his plate, she shoved it into her mouth. "See, not poisoned. I like to play with you, Mac."

His eyes lifted to hers. "Lucky me. Where did you learn to cook?" Shifting the food he had spit from his mouth to the edge of his plate, he stabbed a red pepper.

"From our cook. I used to bug her as a child when I was bored, which was often. So she taught me to cook. She used to say to me, 'Lizzy, no use wasting your life when God gave you a brain and two hands, now cook something.'" Smiling, she took a sip from her glass, remembering all the times she'd stood beside the robust woman and mixed batter or chopped vegetables.

"She taught you well, this is terrific."

"Thank you." She took another forkful of food, paused. "I like your house, Mac." She slipped the fork between her lips, slowly slid it out, watching him as she ate.

He wanted to be that fork. "Meager compared to your standards, I'm sure."

"This is a home; there's love here, I can feel it." It was warm and cozy, and filled her with happiness that he obviously couldn't see.

"We were raised here, my two brothers and I. We had plenty of love, and a hell of a lot of fighting." He smiled, then lifted more food to his mouth.

She doubted that the fights he'd had in his home could compare to the ones she'd had in hers. He seemed to lighten up with the mention of fights with his family and she wondered what it might have been like growing up here, with brothers. "You have two brothers? How nice, I always wanted a sibling." Someone to go to when things got bad. But her mother had stated enough times that one burden of a child had been more than enough, any more would have driven her to insanity. The ride wouldn't have been that far in Liz's opinion.

"They come in handy."

"Where are you in the chain of siblings, Mac?"

"Youngest."

"Ah, the baby. I suppose you were spoiled rotten, too?" She swirled the red liquid in her glass before sipping. She had no idea what it was like to be adored but she'd heard or read enough to understand it. And envy it.

He snickered as he reached for his glass "I was picked on, beaten up and tormented by two older brothers."

"And you love them dearly." She smiled and caught the warmth in his eyes.

"Yeah."

"Is that why you bulked up?" She continued to eat, totally engrossed in learning more about him.

"There was that, and I liked the way the ladies ogled men with muscles." He wiggled one eye brow as he lifted his glass of wine and sipped.

She smiled. "And I'm sure you get plenty of ogling, too." She did enough when he wasn't looking. "What are their names? Your brothers," she clarified.

"Zachary and Sebastian."

"Interesting names."

"Could have been worse. My mother was partial to Ezekiel for me."

"Who persuaded her otherwise?"

"Sebastian, or Bas, as he likes to be called. He loved mac and cheese, when I was born, and told my mother that if I wasn't named Mac he would run away from home."

"I would thank your brother for his love of pasta." She smiled as she set her empty plate aside. Time for business. "I have a proposition for you, Mac."

"Okay, let's hear it."

She pulled out a cigarette, handed it to him, pulled another out for herself. "It wasn't just me that was used; you got a raw deal out of this as well." She held the lighter up to his cigarette.

He took her wrist in his hand to steady the flame and felt her pulse beating against his fingers. Their eyes met and held for a moment before she turned away.

"I figure you risked a great deal bringing me here, to your home. Anyone could have found out. Plus, my father knew just how to get to you. He's good at that, working on a person's needs, faults and such. I suspect he learned of your predicament and persuaded the banks not to grant you the loan." She flicked ashes into the small ashtray beside the bed. "So I figure, you deserve more for your troubles."

"Why are you doing this Liz? Why haven't you called the cops on me yet?"

Shrugging her shoulders, she drew on her cigarette, pulling her feet up on the chair as she spoke. "You're not the one who needs to pay here, Mac."

"I was the one who took you, tied you up and held you here against your will. I think the courts would think differently than you."

Tapping the cigarette in the ashtray, Liz let out a long sigh. "That's why no one will ever find out the truth. Here's what I've decided we're going to do. You are going to call my father and tell him you've had a change of heart and you want more money."

"I have, huh? What makes you think he'll go for that?" He crushed his cigarette out and listened intently to what she said.

"Because he's going to hear me screaming."

His eyes darted to hers. "Now why would you be screaming?"

"You're going to pretend to be slapping me."

Mac's lips twitched with humor. "Right, pretend."

Liz shook her head; she'd left herself open to that one. "Behave, Mac; I'm going to make you a very rich man."

"Oh, do tell."

"You are going to tell my father I am worth more than that paltry amount he'd planned to pay you." She took one last drag from her cigarette before crushing it out.

"How much more?" he asked cautiously, leaning forward.

"Two million." His laughter barreled out fast and loud and gave her a jolt.

"Oh, sure, princess, no problem, I'm sure he'll go for that without question." He shook his head. "You can't be serious?"

She crossed her arms over her chest and leaned back. "I'm perfectly serious. He'll do it, too, because you'll tell him if he doesn't, you'll send a tip to the local papers telling them how he constructed this whole ordeal."

"Princess, Liz, he'll have the cops here faster than you can say boo."

"No, he won't. His career is too precious to him, he won't risk unfavorable publicity." She knew her father very well, he hated looking bad.

"Or his daughter's life."

Liz stood, walked around the bed and grabbed the tray and empty dishes without commenting.

"Haven't you forgotten something?" Mac asked, lifting his free hand.

She turned to him, shrugged. "No. I'm not going to tie you up, but I am going to ask that you stay in here and think over what I've asked. Trust me, Mac, I know what I am doing." She paused, turned back to him. "Do you honestly believe my father would care if I was in danger? He did after all arrange this whole thing in the first place."

"He insisted you not be harmed."

She felt her eyes burning; bit her lip to hold back the tears that threatened to spill out. "But it never occurred to him that I was harmed, by his deception and greed."

"You were never supposed to know he'd arranged this."

Liz turned, her eyes glistening with tears. "And that excuses it all?" She shook her head, shook off the words. "Think about what I said, Mac." She turned back to the door, unlocked it, then slipped out.

Whether I was supposed to know or not is irrelevant now, it's what he did, she thought bitterly. The most important thing to him was not his daughter; it was as always his precious career.

It had never been her.

Chapter 21

Sitting up in his bed, resting against the iron head board, Mac gave Liz's plan serious thought, his mind so focused on everything she'd said that he didn't even think to untie his one remaining hand still attached to the post. What she suggested scared the hell out of him, and he doubted that the old man would go for such an exorbitant amount. But it was her sadness, the tears in her eyes that had his mind working on overtime and his heart aching.

He'd heard around the set of neglect from her parents. He admitted he didn't know that much about Liz other than what the papers said, and most of it unfavorable. But he couldn't get past the sadness he'd heard in her voice.

It was obvious her father thought more of his career than his child; to want publicity at her expense was just cold. Why hadn't he realized that sooner, Mac thought to himself?

Sure the money had been good at the time; now, not so much. He never should have agreed to this in the first place. He had brains, he shouldn't have let dollar signs cloud his mind. But his parents' farm meant so much to him. And at the time, Liz meant nothing to him.

Or, she hadn't when this all had begun.

He owed her this much, and if she wanted some sort of revenge on her father, then he'd help her get it. Even if it meant ending up in jail.

~

Liz wandered through the house, admiring the place Mac called his. There were homey touches everywhere, ornaments that sat on tiny shelves, a sofa that looked well used and comfortable, a floor that wasn't quite polished and showed signs of many feet. And pictures, so many pictures of family. Nothing like the house she'd grown up in. Sterile and cold.

Smiling at the wall of photos, Liz admired Mac's family. *My, my, someone's family had been dealt a wealth of handsome genes.* Liz could see the resemblance in each of Mac's siblings. Though the hair colors were shades different, the facial features were all quite similar. They favored their father a great deal. Liz imagined in his youth, their father been a heart throb. Though in the picture his hair was turning grey and there were wrinkles by his eyes, the elderly man was still a looker. Mac's mother was no slouch in that department, either. She was a beauty with a fall of dark curls around a delicate, sweet face.

And from the looks of it, Mac was the only one without a wife. Smiling, she touched the photo of a happy family portrait. Look at those adorable faces, she thought, what smiles those children have. They were happy, not faking it for a stupid picture, but truly happy. So unlike the family portrait her father orchestrated them to sit for each year. She remembered all the times her father forced her to sit and smile, back straight, chin up, eyes just off of the camera. She'd hated it every damn time.

Shrugging it off, she continued to wander the house. Everything was so clean, and she noticed there wasn't a speck of dust to be seen. Having seen the rest of the house, she deduced that Mac was a tidy man. She doubted he had a maid, he didn't seem the type. So he preferred cleanliness. Had Mac's mother encouraged that in her children?

Her mother hadn't taught her a damn thing. Most of the time her mother couldn't give her even one precious moment of her time, never had. Eliza Cromwell had given birth, but she was no mother. Liz shook the bitterness away.

This house was warm and cozy, and she could easily see herself living here, waking here, sleeping here, and that baffled her more than just a little. It wasn't the smallness of the house, or the lack of servants, she could do without that. She could see herself here, with Mac. *Don't jump too far ahead, Liz, stay in the now.*

She lifted the homemade multi-toned knitted blanket

from the sofa and wrapped it around her body, sighing at the softness. But it didn't hurt to dream just a little.

~

Mac dreamt as well. Holding Liz in his arms, making love to her under a fall of bright sparkling stars. She was soft in his arms, pliant as he touched her delicate skin. And when they joined, her face lit with joy, joy for him. "Mac." She sighed his name. When her hand clamped onto his arm, he spoke softly. "Harder?"

The sharp sting to his arm snapped him out of his dream. His eyes opened and he saw her standing above him. "Shit." He blew out a breath, felt his heart thudding and realized he'd been perilously close to a wet dream.

"What the hell were you dreaming about?"

Smiling, he sat up and rubbed his free hand over his face. "If I told you, you would probably smack me." He took a good look at her now. Her blonde hair hung loosely around her face, her eyes unpainted and she looked like an angel. She wore his mother's handmade blanket around her shoulders and it looked as if it had been made for her.

"So this is how you debate the offer I handed to you, by sleeping?" she said with a bit of a tang to her voice.

"I considered your offer, but put me in a bed and I tend to doze off quickly."

"What a shame," she teased.

God, her eyes were so sexy. The green seemed to sparkle when she teased him. "Well, unless I'm kept occupied, that is. I'm awake now, care to entertain me?"

"What conclusion have you come to in regards to my offer, Mac?"

There's that sophisticated prima donna again. She wore it like a coat she could take off or put back on any time she pleased. "It sounds plausible, but I want something from you in return."

She hugged the blanket to her breast and nodded. "Oh, what is that?"

"I want you to promise that when this is over and

done, that neither you nor your father will charge me or so much as implicate me in this whole fiasco."

"Okay, Mac, I promise nothing will happen to you when this is over."

"Good, there's a small tape recorder in the nightstand by my bed, if you wouldn't mind getting it out and verifying your promise on tape."

"Naturally." She understood his need to protect himself. Grabbing the tiny recorder from his drawer, she held it to her mouth and pressed record. "I, Elizabeth Monique Cromwell, swear that I will never prosecute or so much as reveal Mac —" she paused, clicked stop. "What's your last name?"

"Tyrell."

"Hmm, Mac Tyrell. Just doesn't have a ring to it."

"It's Mackenzie, actually," he supplied.

Mackenzie Tyrell, she liked it. She pressed record. "Mackenzie Tyrell's involvement in my abduction. And as long as I live and breathe, I will see to it that my father, Jonathan Cromwell, refrains from doing him harm as well." She pressed stop and smiled with complete sweetness. "Good?"

"Perfect, now can you date it, vocally?" He wasn't taking any chances.

Still smiling, she pressed record one more time. "Today's date is July fifteenth, two thousand and seven." She pressed stop. "Better?"

"Much, now pop the tape out and snap off the tab."

"Don't you trust me, Mac?"

"Just covering my ass, princess. It's your father I don't trust."

"And might I add what a fine ass it is." She slipped the tape out, popped the tab then set it beside him on the bed. "Now, your decision?"

"You like my ass, huh?"

She blushed, looking down for a moment. "Let's stick to the subject for a moment, shall we?"

"I don't know, a change of pace might be nice." He gave her a teasing look.

"What's your answer, Mac?"

"I've decided to go along with your plan." He knew she wasn't unaffected by his charm, the sultry look in her eyes told volumes.

The excitement slipped into her eyes first, then she let out a loud cheer and clapped her hands. "I just knew you wouldn't be able to resist the cash."

He shook his head clear, mesmerized by the beauty in her eyes. "It wasn't the cash, though that is a nice incentive, but there's something more important."

"Oh, and what might that be?"

"You."

"Me?"

"Your father is slime, and I'm sorry I didn't see that before. Anyone who would do this to their own child is sick and deserves to pay. Since going to the police isn't an option unless I want to serve time, milking him of his money will have to do. So anything you want to do to him, I'll go along with, because you deserve your revenge."

"I wouldn't let you go to jail, Mac," she said on a sigh.

He tilted his head. "You sound like you actually mean that."

"I told you, you were used as well."

"Yeah, true, but doesn't a part of you want to make me suffer for my involvement?"

"You're tied to the bed, aren't you?" she said wickedly.

He lifted his free hand, giving it a shake. "Am I?"

Damn, it completely slipped her mind that she'd left one hand free. "Why haven't you untied the other one?"

He shrugged wide shoulders. "Maybe I'm into bondage." A warm sensation filled his chest, seeing her wrapped in his mother's blanket. "That looks good on you."

She stroked the blanket, snuggling into it. "It's very

soft and beautiful."

"My mother made it."

"Well, she does wonderful work." She stood, backing away from the bed.

"She did. She passed away a few years ago." He could untie himself, but he waited for the perfect opportunity.

"I'm sorry. So it's just you and your brothers, then?"

"Yep." He sat up a bit more, smiling to himself when he saw her eyes widen.

"Why don't they live here instead of you?" She backed to the door.

"They aren't the farm type. I took over when my father's health got too bad for him to continue caring for it."

"Do they know you're close to losing it?"

"No. They're just starting out with their own families; I couldn't tell them how bad it is." He shifted and saw her inch a little more towards the door.

"Will you tell them how you got the money to keep it, should they find out?"

He paused, the guilt sliding into him once again. "No. Are you afraid of me, Liz?"

Her quick burst of laughter caught him off guard. "Never."

His brow lifted. "Then why are you backing away from me now?"

"Because I don't trust that you won't tie me back up."

His laughter caught her off guard. "I would never do that."

"Oh, you would, in a heart beat."

Mac's lips curved up as he moved his free hand to the one tied to the post. "Maybe before, but not now."

She watched, holding her breath as he released the knots around his wrist. "What is so different now?"

His eyes turned to her, showing her the softer side. "You're not the same person I thought you were once." He slid from the bed and moved closer to her.

She bumped into the door, feeling caged and not too sure what to expect. "Is that so?" she said breathlessly.

"Definitely." Like he had once before, he pressed her to the door, his hands caging her in, his eyes looking into hers with dreamy wantonness. "I might have thought you were a snob once, but not now. I was wrong to assume that," he said as he moved his mouth closer to her. "Am I wrong, now, thinking you want me to kiss you?"

She closed her eyes, let her body relax. "No."

"I want you, Liz."

"I know," she said breathlessly, swallowing hard.

He backed away, and that took a great deal out of him. "But I won't push you, not until you're ready."

Her eyes opened slowly. "You're just chicken, Mac."

His brow lifted. "I'm chicken?"

"Yep." She opened the door and sauntered down the stairs.

"I'm chicken?"

"And, apparently, hard of hearing." She smiled as she stepped into the kitchen, grabbing his cigarette pack.

"And why is it I'm chicken, princess?"

She turned to him, her long blonde hair falling over her shoulders, and she smiled. "Because you've never had a real woman like me before, and you haven't a clue what to do with me."

"Oh, princess, I have plenty in mind to do with you." And as she stepped through the patio doors to his back yard, he began imagining all the things he could do to her. Smiling, he headed out after her.

Chapter 22

The sun sat low in the horizon, and he realized he'd spent the better part of a glorious day tied to his bed. But he knew, had she not tied him to the bed, things wouldn't have turned out as they were now. So it all worked out for the best. He hoped.

"I love your yard, Mac."

"Thanks." He watched her light a cigarette, then caught the pack as she tossed it over her back. "I've got plans for it."

"Such as?"

He tucked the lighter in his shirt pocket after lighting his cigarette, then hurried to catch up to her. "Well, my dream has always been to start up a horse ranch."

She turned to him, her eyes wide. "Horses? Yes, yes, I can see it now." She turned back to the vast property before her. "There will be a corral out there and dozens of horses grazing in the field. And the baby horses will be playing while their mothers nourish themselves for another feed."

He smiled at her vision. "They're called foals."

"I know that," she said quickly, her mind still envisioning the horses in the field. "Why haven't you started it up yet?"

"Money. They want it, I don't have it."

She turned to him now, flicking the ashes to the ground. "Well, after this, you'll have plenty."

"We'll see. What is this going to do to your relationship with your father, Liz?"

She shrugged elegant shoulders and moved out past the terrace and onto the soft grass. The blades of grass tickled her bare feet. "We've never had a relationship."

"You know what I mean."

She paused, turned to him. "If my father gave a damn about my feelings, he wouldn't have done this to me, so your answer is, it can't get any worse."

That saddened him a great deal. "And your mother?"

Dropping the cigarette on the ground, ready to crush it with her foot when she realized her feet were bare "I don't know that she isn't involved in this."

He stomped it out for her, then his as well. "He never mentioned her knowing. Are the two of you close?"

"Hardly," she admitted with a faint chuckle. "You ever have an acquaintance that you know, but not well enough to be comfortable with?"

"I suppose so."

"That is my mother."

"Get real, Liz."

She turned to him with absolute seriousness. "She reminded me constantly that I was a burden to her and if she hadn't been accidentally impregnated by my father, she would never have had children."

His heart lodged in his throat. "My God."

The pity in his voice made her ache. "Tell me more about your plans for the horse ranch."

Appalled that she had such horrible parents, he understood her need to drop the subject. "I thought I would start out with a few, breed them, and go from there."

"Will you sell them, race them, what?"

"Sell them, mostly, as racers." He reached out to touch her golden hair. She turned to him and smiled and his heart was gone. In the setting sun, her face was more than radiant, and he knew he could never let her go. "Liz—"

"I think it will be perfect. You have so much land here, plenty of room for them to run. I think it would be fun to train them."

"You mean, watch someone train them?"

She turned to him, a frown on her lips. "I think it might be interesting to learn how to work with them."

"And get those delicate fingers of yours dirty?"

She turned with fire in her eyes. Bending down, she scooped up a handful of dirt and held it out to him. "They're only delicate because I've never felt the need to dirty them. But things change." She dumped the dirt at his feet and turned to walk away.

Yes, she was right, and he felt like a heel for assuming something of her that might not be true. "Have you ever ridden a horse, Liz?"

"Yes, Mac, I have. Have you?" she replied with playful sarcasm.

"I was one of the main stunt men on the movie *Back to the West*, two years ago. You know, the one where the two preppie lawyers are thrown back in time and have to learn to live as cowboys?"

"It sounds familiar, but I don't think I saw it. Hmm, I wonder what other movies I might have seen with you in them." She plucked up a stray blade of grass as she walked along the yard.

"I could show you my portfolio some time."

"How long have you been a stunt man?"

It amazed her that she wasn't even walking on tip toes over the rough terrain. "I started just out of high school, so twelve years, give or take."

"What made you decide to become a stunt man?" She tucked the blade of grass between her teeth.

She looked absolutely perfect. "My parents informed me that I had one month to find a lucrative job or they'd ship me off to join the Army. I was a bit of a trouble maker in my youth."

"Get out, you, a trouble maker?" She snorted, then smiled coyly.

He'd walked into that one. "I took a job with a construction company and, long story short, I met a guy who knew a guy who said I would be perfect for a role in his movie. And here I am now."

"And here you are, back at home. Will you still work as a stunt man after you start your ranch?"

"No, I hope to retire from the movie biz."

"Well it looks as if that will come to fruition soon enough. This is a beautiful stretch of land; I would have fought tooth and nail to keep it as well."

"Oh, this is nothing, I have something much better to show you. Care to see it?"

"Sure."

"Then come with me." Taking her hand in his, he led her along. "Want me to carry you?"

"I'm more than capable of walking, Mac."

There was that quick wit again. "That's true, but you're barefoot, and the terrain is a little bumpy."

She looked down, noticing her bare feet. "Been a while since I felt dirt between my toes. I think I might like it. Where are you taking me, Mac?"

"To my secret hide-away." He moved low-lying tree branches for her as they walked along the path he'd taken so many times before.

"Is it far?"

"Nope." He stopped her short, taking her other hand in his. "We're here."

"We are?" Looking around, she saw nothing but trees. "This is your secret hiding place Mac, a bunch of trees? How ingenious." She snorted with a roll of her eyes.

He loved the way she did that. "Shut up, Liz." Taking her head in his hands, he did what he'd longed to do for days. Touched his lips to hers.

As the leaves on the trees rustled around them, they embraced. The kiss that had been in the making for days came to them finally in a play of raw emotion. Her hands lifted to touch his hair as she angled for the kiss.

Still holding her head in his hands, he watched as her eyes fluttered open. The green seemed to glaze over and the blonde lashes fluttered as she tried to resurface. She kissed like a dream.

"Well, princess, are you ready?"

"Oh, God, yes," she panted, more than ready.

Smiling, Mac tilted her head up. "Then start climbing."

Chapter 23

"You want me to climb up this tree?"

He snickered behind her back, his hands resting on her hips, his face nuzzled in her hair. It smelled like apple blossoms. "Yep, ever climbed a tree before, princess?"

"As it so happens, Mac, yes I have."

He snorted in response.

Her head angled over her shoulder and she sent him a chilled look. "There's this huge oak tree just outside my window, much like the one outside your bedroom window, the one you said I would have a long fall from if I tried to escape." He looked down sheepishly and she continued. "I've shimmied up and down that tree for years, sneaking out of my room."

"You rebel you," he teased, having a great deal of respect for her knowing that. "But I prefer action over words. Show me you can climb a tree."

Shaking her head, she took the steps up the tree.

Mac watched with amazement as she shimmied up the tree with no problem.

At the top, she climbed into the wooden tree house, then turned to him. With a smug look on her face, she held her hand out to him. "Do you need a hand, Mac?"

He shook his head, then hurried up the wooden steps. "Funny girl."

"So was this your hide-away as a child?"

"Yeah, as a child." He grinned slyly as he sat down beside her. He liked watching her absorb things; it was fascinating to watch, and sad all at the same time. What had her life been like as a child? "I still come here when I want to escape." He caught the glint in her eyes, placed his hands on her shoulders and turned her to the window. "For the view."

Her breath caught as she looked through the square opening designed as a window and saw the beautiful scene before her. Tall rugged mountains with snow capped tips sparkled in the low sunlight. "It's breath taking."

"Isn't it, though?" He'd never shared it with any other woman before, until now. "Ever been rock climbing, Liz?" He watched her as she drank in the beauty of the mountains before her. Like watching a child marvel at a new toy.

"No, and I can't say I'm too eager to try it, either. Let me guess, you have?"

He toyed with the ends of her hair; it felt like silky gold. "My family used to climb once a year. I haven't done it in years, though." He hadn't realized how much he missed it until now.

"Why not?" His fingers skimmed through her hair, touching the back of her neck, making her shiver.

"I've been busy working and taking care of my father."

"What did he die of? If you don't mind me asking?" she asked, breathlessly as she leaned into his hands.

"Colon cancer."

"How sad."

Their eyes met and hers seem to say to him, *touch me now, love me.* And he found he wanted just that. His lips curved up as his hand cupped the back of her neck to pull her to him. She sunk into his lips, melting like cotton candy, leaving him with the sweetness of sugar behind.

While his lips drank hers in, his hands sculpted the form of her body. She shivered when his hands moved over her, sliding down from her shoulders, down over her arms, then stopping. Then, when he moved his hands from her arms to just below her breast, her breath caught. "Do you want me to stop?"

"No."

With a quick tug he pulled her tight against him, and she let out a gasp. Her breasts pressed against his chest and with each breath they rose and fell. His hands worked under her shirt to caress her back, the smooth silkiness of her skin, the lines and muscles beneath.

She quivered for him; he wanted her shaking. When his lips left her mouth to trail over her cheek, down to her chin, she tipped her head back to give him easier access.
"I've wanted this for so long."

"Me, too," she moaned.

Slowly, torturously slowly, he lifted the shirt over her head. Her upper torso was bare all but for the tiny excuse of a lacy white bra, and nothing could have turned him on more. He kissed her soft round shoulders, taking his time as he slid his mouth down to her chest. She panted for him; he wanted her breathless. His tongue slid out and trailed down the length of exposed cleavage. She had an erotic taste, and a very addictive one. She gasped; he pulled away. "Too fast?"

"Not fast enough." She panted and smiled when he continued his seduction.

Liz was expecting him to be fast, so he purposely slowed down. He couldn't resist, however, the feel of her hot skin next to his, and removed his shirt. He lowered them to the cool wooden floor, wishing now he'd kept a blanket near.

Her hands on his arms were soft, the way she squeezed the muscles were not. He could feel the need in her, wanting him to relieve her of her ache but he took it easy. He wanted to draw it out for as long as he could.

Her back arched as he skimmed his hand along her belly, saying to him, *take me, for God sake's, take me now*.

Lifting her hips, she wiggled and he knew he could take her right now, in one swift thrust and please them both. But he wanted more, and he wanted to give her more. Unsnapping the button on her slacks, he felt her breath hitch. When he lowered the zipper, her breath sucked in with anticipation. Her hips wiggled in invitation, but he merely slid the slacks down slowly.

Kicking her slacks away, Liz begged him with her hands, with her body, to give her satisfaction, yet still he didn't. His hands slid over her body, leaving the needy parts untouched. He removed his pants while his mouth kissed, while his tongue danced with hers. He felt the scrape of her teeth on his bottom lip and it sent shivers coursing though him. Her chest heaved, her breasts rose in invitation as he moved over her. But still he waited.

He hovered over her, giving her just a sample of what she could expect when he penetrated her, but he wasn't quite close enough to satisfy. She dug her nails into his back and urged him lower and he nearly gave in and took her then and there.

She moved so erotically, so much so he needed to bite down on his lip to prevent himself from losing control. He wanted to make her squirm, make her want him, need only him. But he knew if she kept up those gyrations it would push him over the edge. So he released her lips and sat back on his knees. She looked so incredible, with that lusty look on her face.

"My God, look at you."

"And look at you." Lowering, he tasted the sweet salt of the sweat that had built up over her body from their mutual heat. His fingers barely touched her as he unclasped the lacy bra and let it fall to the side. Her scrumptious looking full breasts fell free, begging him to touch them.

Her hands urged him lower, to sample, to taste, to have. And when his mouth came down to nibble on her breast, she let out a gasp and lifted for him to drink his fill. His tongue teased, flicked, his teeth scraped, bit, she arched and he felt her body tremble in response.

"Oh, God." The tears slid down the sides of her face to wet her hair, and she smiled. "Now, Mac, now."

He couldn't resist it any longer and quickly removed the restrictions between them. She opened for him, drew him down, and pulled him in deep. She was like liquid fire, warming him, coating him in her heat. She was silky wetness wrapped in heaven meant to smother. Her warmth clasped tightly onto him and sucked him in, and he knew,

Kidnapped

like never before, he'd fallen over the edge of no return.

Like a volcanic explosion, she erupted, smothering him with heat and fire and slowly killing him with desire. He'd never felt a woman climax like Liz before, and his body reacted in the most incredible way. Lifting her hips high, he plunged, grunting as his body convulsed and drove them both over the edge.

The sun set behind the mountain as their bodies quivered with release.

Chapter 24

"Dear God," he panted. "Wow!"

Her body felt so content, maybe for the fist time in her entire life. "Thank you."

"Aren't we smug?"

"I could learn to be." She nuzzled into his arm and kissed his muscular chest. She could live here, right here in the comfort of his arms and never want for anything ever again. Then she opened her eyes and she saw the darkness.

The air seemed to be sucked from her lungs. Bolting upright, she panicked as she searched the smothering darkness for an escape "We need to get back."

"What's the hurry?"

"It's getting dark." Finding her bra, she slipped it back on and did it up, then searched for her underwear. Her chest ached from lack of breath; her head began to spin.

"We could make love under the moon." He teased a finger along her bare foot and felt her flinch. "Liz?"

"Inside sounds better." *Where there are lights, lots of bright burning lights.*

"What's wrong?"

"It's chilly, I need to get back, I'm cold," she lied, her eyes darting around the darkened tree house.

"Okay, okay, we'll head back." He dressed in a hurry.

"Damn it, damn it, I can't breathe." Oh, God, why did her zipper have to catch now when she needed so badly to hurry?

"Relax, Liz, just relax." He touched her shoulder, she jumped. "Liz, what's wrong?"

"It's dark." She hadn't been fast enough, now the light had gone and she couldn't breathe. The darkness had long, nimble fingers that wrapped around her throat to squeeze the air from her lungs. She tried to swallow and found she couldn't.

He stepped into her view, cupping her chin in his

hand. "Are you afraid of the dark, Liz?"

Her breath came out fast, short, and labored. "Terrified." Her heart pounded so hard she felt her body shaking. She wouldn't let it get her, yet she felt as if the darkness closed in on her. It was everywhere, sneaking up on her, sneaking into her.

"Okay, I'm right here." He rubbed her arms, trying to get some warmth back into her skin. "I have a flash light up here, let me just get it, then we can head back to the house. Just stay calm Liz, slow your breathing."

She moved with him, clinging to his arm, never more grateful for light as she was now when he clicked the flashlight on, illuminating the tiny room. The air rushed into her lungs and burnt like fire. The darkness wouldn't get her now, she was safe.

"Better?"

"A little." It was still dark outside. "I should have been paying more attention." She felt foolish now. She didn't want people knowing about her phobia and had successfully kept it a secret for years.

He rubbed her arm with one hand while the other held the flashlight. "We were a little preoccupied."

She nodded, her eyes fixed on the darkness. "It's so dark out there." It looked as if they'd stepped into a void of space. Nothing to mar the darkness, to split it up. It was out there, waiting for her to step near it so it could smother her.

"Liz, look at me. We have the flashlight, see, light. Come on, why don't you hold the flashlight while I help you down?"

She only nodded and grabbed hold of it as if it was her life line.

"Okay, wrap your legs around my waist and hang onto my neck while I back down."

She only nodded and climbed onto his back. Wrapping her arms around his neck, her legs around his waist, she held the flashlight in a tight grip as he carried her down.

"Okay, we're down, are you okay?" He jumped down from the last step.

She clung to him and just stared into the beam of the light. Though it made her eyes water, she couldn't afford to look away. "No, and I hate admitting that." Even with the flashlight she knew the darkness waited for her, circling around her, waiting to smother her.

"Everyone has some sort of fear."

"I've tried so hard to keep that a secret from people." She kept her eyes focused on the beam of light, not even realizing he carried her as he walked through the woods.

"Why hide it?"

"I'm a grown woman with an utter fear of the dark, you don't think the tabloids would exploit that, or some sicko would be out to get me?"

"I see your point." He shifted her and kept walking. "How long have you had this fear?"

The branches crunched beneath his feet like a far off echo in her head. Her mind focused on the light in her hand. "All my life."

"Must be difficult for you. When did it begin?"

She didn't even realize she leaned her cheek on his hair, or that she'd begun to relax. "I used to have horrible nightmares as a child; my nanny used to berate me and tell me to grow up and that she was tired of me bawling my brains out. When she caught me sneaking out of bed after she'd left to turn the light on, she removed the bulbs from my room. When I pleaded and cried for her to give me some light, she would threaten me with solitary confinement. She took her threats seriously, as I found out soon enough. When she meant business, she meant business. Her favorite form of punishment was locking me in this small cubby hole inside my closet, used for shoes." Her body tensed with the memory of it. She could still feel the panic she felt back then, trying to push the door, begging to have it opened, the darkness surrounding her, tiny bugs crawling on her skin.

He stopped dead in his tracks and shifted her so he could look into her face. "Why in God's name didn't your parents have her fired?"

"As long as I was dealt with and out of their hands, they were happy." She remembered quite painfully, telling her mother what her nanny had done and her mother's response. *"Darling, if you learn to obey you won't be punished."* No sympathy from her mother whatsoever. That was when she'd learned she had no one to rely on. At the tender age of five.

"God, Liz, I am so sorry."

"Why? You didn't do it."

He shifted his head and met her eyes. "I'm sorry I took part in your father's sick scheme, if I'd known—"

She placed a finger to his lips and stopped his words. "You didn't, how could you?"

"But still—"

Bending over his shoulder, she stopped him with an awkwardly placed kiss. "Don't go getting all weepy on me, Mac. If none of this had ever happened I might never have realized what a vile man my father really is." She kissed him again. "In a sense, I have you to thank for that."

"Please don't."

"Let's finish this, Mac, you and I, and show him what it's like to suffer."

"I don't know, Liz, I—"

"Mac." She kissed his cheek to quiet him. "I don't want to put you in a place that you're not comfortable with, but I know my father. He won't let this go. When he finds out the deal is off, he'll get nasty and he won't take the worst of it out on me. It's you he'll bury, trust me. I don't want that to happen."

"Okay Liz, you've got a deal." He dropped her to her feet.

Liz looked down at the cool pavement beneath her feet, then up at Mac and realized her arms wound around his neck, her face in his hair. "You carried me?"

Smiling, he turned her to face him and kissed her lightly on the nose. "Yes, princess, I did."

The light shimmered all around her, bright brilliant light from the overhead patio lanterns. "Why?"

"You have a death grip," he joked with her, putting his hands on her arms.

She suddenly realized her hands were sore and pulled them, with great effort, from around his neck. "Oh, God, I'm sorry. Did I hurt you?"

"No, Liz, you didn't hurt me."

"Good. Home sweet home." She muttered as she entered through the terrace doors into the kitchen. "Let's cook together. I found these wonderful steaks in your freezer earlier and I'm dying to—" She turned to see him standing in the doorway, a blank stare in his eyes. "What?"

"Nothing."

She angled her head. "No, it's definitely something." Her hand rested on the table as she looked up at him with determination. "You don't think I consider this homey, you don't think I fit here, do you Mac?" He still didn't know her, and that hurt.

He lifted the pack of cigarettes from his pocket, pulled one out and lit it up. "It's just a little hard for me to picture you in front of a stove cooking, or scrubbing floors for that fact."

She stole the cigarette from him, annoyed. "How can I change your opinion of me then?" she asked with a bit of a snap in her voice, then sucked on the cigarette, her eyes blazing.

"Well, you can start by cooking dinner; I would love to see that." He stole the cigarette back, laid it between his lips and let the smoke linger.

"Fine, I'll show you I can be Miss Domestic." She stole the cigarette back, took a drag.

"It was sheer luck that you threw that concoction together earlier, because anyone that can actually cook wouldn't have left the kitchen in this sort of mess."

"Luck? I'll have you know, pal, I am a damn good cook, and the only reason why the kitchen is still a mess is because I was concentrating on getting you to agree with my plan."

"Uh huh." Grabbing the cigarette from her fingers, he backed away, preventing her from taking it back.

"You don't believe me?"

"Its okay, princess, it's not that big of a deal."

"Not that big of a deal?" She huffed. "Well, I'll show you, Mackenzie Tyrell. Back off and let me work," she insisted with her eyes staring him down.

Hands in the air, he did as she demanded.

Chapter 25

Okay, so the woman knew how to cook. Mac took a chair and watched as she prepped the steaks in a marinade of lemon juice, salt and pepper. While they marinated, she chopped up a few potatoes, set them in a pan with oil, seasoned them, then covered them and let them simmer. The steaks went on the grill and into the oven and then she turned to the dishes and began washing them.

She searched his cupboards for what she needed and all while looking like a goddamn pro. Elizabeth Cromwell had just proven to him that she was most definitely Miss Domestic.

Lifting his head, he saw the smile on her face. "Enjoying yourself, aren't you?"

"Absolutely. You look cute when you pout."

"I'm not pouting."

"Funny, that's just what it looks like to me, big guy. Here, make yourself useful and put out the plates."

He took the plates she held out to him as well as the cutlery and set them on the table. Seeing the effort she put into cooking for him—and proving him wrong—he decided it called for something a bit more. Opening the pantry doors, he pulled out two slim crystal candleholders that had always been his mother's favorite and set them on the table. Pulling out his lighter, he lit the candles. He dimmed the lights, catching her attention.

"What are you doing?"

"Creating a mood."

She didn't have to be told to know what that mood was. "How sweet."

"I have my moments." Spotting a vase of flowers on the counter, he set them on the table between the candles. He wasn't sure how they got there but assumed Liz had picked them earlier.

"You certainly do, and that was one of the things that drew me to you," she commented casually as she pulled the steaks from the oven.

"Do you have any idea how many times my mind wandered to kissing you?" Lifting the bottle of wine, he poured them each a glass of wine.

She turned with the plate of steaks, setting them on the table, smiling slyly. "Probably as many times as mine did."

"Was it everything you expected?"

"Need your ego stroked, big guy?" She set the potatoes on the table, smirking. "Yes, and so much more. Dinner is served."

He took her hands in his, capturing her eyes. "You astound me, princess, thank you."

"Mac," she sighed.

"Now, let's see if it's as good as it smells." Releasing her, he held the chair, waiting as she took the seat.

"Oh, this is incredible," he said after cutting into his steak and taking a bite.

"Thank you."

"Okay, so you can cook, and you managed to do a good job cleaning up after yourself, but I have to know something. How the hell did you manage to get me on the bed and tie me up?"

Smiling proudly, Liz speared a potato with her fork. "It wasn't easy, but I was motivated, so I pushed myself. You're not light, you know."

"You're a woman of many talents."

"You don't know the half of it."

His body warmed to the way she purred that statement. "Yeah?" The ringing phone startled him. "Damn phone," Scooping it up, he saw the name on the I.D. and his eyes shot to hers. "It's him."

"Him?"

Mac waved his hand at the phone, as if that would help any. "Your father."

"Oh my God. Blow him off, we aren't ready." She jumped up and moved in beside Mac, the ringing phone making her nervous.

"Blow him off, how exactly should I do that?" God, his hands were clammy. Why now was he so damn nervous to talk to the guy?

"I don't know, figure it out, and make it quick." She motioned to the ringing phone.

"Fuck." Mac took a deep breath, then answered. "Tyrell."

"*How are things going?*" Jonathan asked.

"Funny you should ask that," Mac turned his back to Liz, inspiration suddenly hitting him. "I've been doing some thinking, Cromwell." He waved his hand when Liz whispered her protest.

"*Oh, have you now.*"

"Yes, I have, and I figure, your daughter's worth more that two hundred thousand dollars. Much more. I want two million." He waited for the backlash, praying that Liz was right.

The laughter rang through the telephone loud enough for Liz to hear it.

"*That's rich, Tyrell, really rich.*"

He moved away when Liz came up behind him, grabbing his shirt, urging him to hang up. "I want the two million in two days, or I go to the tabloids with my story." He pushed her off and received a nasty scowl and a few choice words under her breath.

"*Please, boy, who do you think they will believe?*"

"Me," Mac pulled out a cigarette, lit it casually, ignoring Liz's fierce eyes. "I have proof. I've recorded every conversation we've ever had," he pressed record on his answering machine, just to be safe. "And I have Terry as a witness." He played the part so easily no one would know to look at him that his legs shook and his knees were weak.

"*Let me speak to my daughter.*"

Mac blew the smoke high above his head, smiled. "Why, so you can tell her what you've done?"

Kidnapped

"I want to know she hasn't been harmed."

"Oh, now you're concerned. Where was that concern when you approached me with this whole idea in the first place? Where was your concern when I told you she wasn't feeling well, Cromwell?"

"I trusted you, we had an agreement, Tyrell. You were only to hold her for a week, then release her unharmed, there was no reason to be concerned."

Mac shook his head. *Did it occur to you that it might traumatize her, you asshole?* "You're not a very bright man, Cromwell. You just said enough to implicate yourself, and I got it all on tape. You have my demands, two days, Cromwell, no more." He ended the call with a snap and turned to see Liz with her mouth hanging open. "Okay, I know, I messed up, it wasn't how we planned it to go, but I just couldn't resist." He crushed his cigarette out and waited for the back lash.

She flew into his arms, wrapped her legs around his waist, nearly toppling them both over, and planted a very loud, sloppy kiss to his lips. "You were incredible, so stern, so demanding. You made me shake. I imagine my father's probably downing a Cognac right now. He does that when he's nervous." She kissed him again. "I feel so, so, invigorated." She bounced on him, her face lit with excitement as she clung to his body.

"Yeah, uh, I'm feeling a little something right now myself."

She caught the gleam in his eyes, the quick intake of air, the shaky breath he let out and the thudding of his heart beat against her chest. Then she felt his hard on jabbing her. "Really?" She trailed her nail along the opening of his shirt, felt him quiver. "Care to explore that feeling a bit further?" She was feeling rather turned on herself.

"Try and stop me." He carried her up the flight of stairs to his room. She giggled the whole time while nibbling on his ear.

He dropped her on the bed, and she gasped when he tore off his shirt. Her body lit with excitement at the rippling muscles in his arms and on his chest, "Be forceful with me, Mac," she tore her own shirt away. "I want it fast."

"Yeah?" He grabbed her by the waist, undid her slacks slowly, then with one hard tug, yanked them down. "Like that?"

"Oh God, yes, more." She felt giddy with lust.

"More?" He removed his pants and pushed her down on the bed. "More?" With two fingers, he flicked the bra open, pushed it away to expose her bare pink and very aroused nipples. "You want more?"

She felt like she might explode, even before he touched her. "Yes, God yes, Mac, now." He shocked her when he tore her panties away, her body quivering with anticipation. He yanked her legs apart, then dove in with his mouth, sending her over the edge.

She let out a scream as he penetrated her with his fingers, her body pulsating with a ripple of sensations. Pleasure, pain, lust and fear. Her hands dug into the sheets, twisted them around her fingers. Her back arched, she lifted, and he plunged even deeper. Her vision blurred as the orgasm shocked her system.

"Still want more?"

"Yes, yes, and fast." She clawed at him, bringing him up, her hips lifting, begging for more. She ached in places she never ached before and it felt glorious. Her body trembled with need, and the thought of him giving her more nearly sent her over the top.

"You want it fast, and hard?"

"Yes." She panted, her body pressing to his with a need that she would have begged to have sated.

He plunged, she gasped, the sensation greater than either knew how to handle. "More?"

Breathless, she knew what she wanted. "Yes, yes."

He pumped his hips harder, faster, until their bodies

glistened with sweat. The bed rocked, the iron headboard clanking with each thrust. She clawed at him, a crazed woman; the wild look in her eyes spoke volumes.

They tossed and turned, he on top, they rolled, she on top. They continued to roll over the bed, mussing the sheets, enjoying the passion, the hunger that enveloped them, the need that threatened to take them over, until their bodies rippled with one vibration after another.

When she felt the orgasm starting to build, she thought she was prepared for it. But then it struck her with such wild abandonment, it took her by surprise.

"Oh…My…God," she screamed, arching up, giving him easier access to enter her deeper.

Grabbing hold of her hips, he let himself go completely.

Exhausted, they both collapsed.

After the daze of sex cleared from her eyes, Liz saw the condition of the bed. "We messed up the bed," she panted with a giggle, her hand resting on her chest.

"I hadn't noticed."

"Do we have to move?" She wasn't too sure she could if she tried. Everything inside of her ached, satisfyingly, the outside of her throbbed pleasantly.

"Only this far." He pulled her into his arms, kissed her head. "How's that?"

"Perfect." Her head rested on his shoulder, one leg swung over his, her hand playing with the tiny dark hairs on his chest. She wanted to stay like this forever. "Now that I've caught my breath, tell me what my father said?"

He toyed with her fingers, slipped one into his mouth and flicked it with his tongue. "He wasn't impressed."

"Good, he hates ultimatums." He was managing to arouse her when she was sure she couldn't possibly feel arousal again anytime soon.

"I'm not too sure it will work."

Lifting her head, her hair sweeping over her face, she pushed it aside and she saw the doubt on his face. "It'll work, Mac. He won't want the negative publicity."

"How did you manage to turn out so normal with—excuse my language—unfeeling, cold hearted pricks like your parents?"

Well, that was blunt, and her heart swam with love. "I am hardly normal, Mac." She looked down, embarrassed.

He lifted her chin, looked sincerely into her eyes. "I thought you were a spoiled rich brat, Liz, one that got whatever she wanted, when she wanted, how she wanted." He sat up, taking her with him, holding her hands in his. "What's inside," he placed his hand over her heart, "is who you are, and that person is a beautiful, headstrong, and perfectly normal young woman."

Her eyes shimmered with warm tears. "No one has ever said anything filled with as much meaning to me before in my life." And she wanted so badly to tell him she loved him. But would he just laugh at her and tell her it was only the heat of the moment, his touching words, and not meant? She couldn't risk it. So she would tuck her love for him into her heart and keep it there where it was warm and safe.

"Maybe they never really took the time to see who you really were."

Liz touched his face, her hand pouring out the love she felt, unknown to him. "Can we stay like this forever, Mac?" Because she was so afraid that when the sun came up, he would go his way and she would go hers. She didn't want that to ever happen.

Smiling, Mac wiped the hair from her face. "We'll have to eat eventually, but I'm good until at least noon tomorrow."

She rested her head on his chest. It hadn't been quite what she meant, but for now it would have to do. "You're making breakfast."

"Deal, if you promise to be waiting right here, naked, when I get back."

Her teary eyes twinkled with a smile. "I suppose I

could manage that." She closed her eyes and wished that daylight never came.

Chapter 26

Wrapped in each other's arms, the sunlight peering in through the blinds on the window, neither Liz nor Mac heard the car pulling up the driveway. Even the first knock on the door went unheard. It wasn't until the knocking turned to a more persistent banging that they stirred.

"What the hell is that?" Liz grumbled as she pulled the blankets over her head, trying to drown out the annoying noise.

"Someone's at the door, I'll take a look out the window." Running a hand over his face, he slipped naked from the bed, tripped over his pants, cursed, then wandered to the window. "Oh, shit."

"What?" One eye peered over the covers, smiling; she admired the firm muscles in Mac's tight bronzed naked body. Yes, the man definitely had a nice ass. "Oh, now I could look at that all day."

He was oblivious to her comment. "Party's over, princess, Daddy's here." Grabbing his pants, Mac hurried into them.

"What?" She sat up, her eyes wide.

"Your father is here," Mac said a little slower, jamming his arms into the sleeves of his shirt.

"Fuck." She tossed the blankets aside, stood up and shielded her eyes from the light.

"Such an eloquent vocabulary for a lady. I guess its time to face the firing squad."

She frowned, chewing her lip, thinking. "Ignore him."

"Does it sound like he's going away any time soon?" The banging only got louder.

"No, damn him." Impatient hands wound through her hair. "Now what do we do?"

Mac ran his hands through his hair, thinking. "You wait here; I'll go down and figure it out as I go." Leaning in, he kissed her quickly. "When this is done, princess, we aren't."

Kidnapped

Liz placed a finger to her lips, could still feel the warmth of Mac's kiss. His words rang through her, warmed her. She knew he didn't mean just today, but tomorrow and after. How much after she couldn't be sure.

Opening Mac's closet, she found a robe in deep blue. Slipping into it, she hugged herself and inhaled his scent still on the robe. Taking a deep breath, she opened the door and listened.

~

Wiping the hair from his face, Mac casually walked to the door; taking a deep breath, he opened it. Jonathan stood before him, dressed in a high class expensive black suit; his sandy hair was, as always, meticulously combed back from his strong boned and aging face. Despite the work he'd had done on it—the rumors ran wild with how much work the guy had done on himself—he still looked old. The urge to pop him in that sophisticated nose of his, tempted Mac, but he held back. *Okay, Tyrell, keep it together.*

"Cromwell, what the hell are you doing here?"

"We need to talk."

Mac snarled at his back as Jonathan pushed his way into the house, closing the door with a snap. "Only if you've come to pay me what I asked for." Following him into the kitchen, Mac cringed as he caught sight of the table, and their left over meal from the night before. Damn it.

"I see you and Orsini have been eating well."

The guy always used a persons' last name as if it were beneath him. Mac was thankful that Cromwell thought it had been Terry that had eaten with him. "It's my money, unless you care to reimburse me?"

"I think not." Jonathan turned to Mac with disgust. "I have no intensions of paying you anything."

"Don't ask how your daughter's doing or anything, I mean, she's nothing right?" He let the clip of bitterness slide smoothly from his lips; his eyes however, aimed to kill. Mac shoved his hands in his pockets to keep them from popping the guy in the face. He really wanted to smack him, knowing the sadness Liz felt, not just from this ordeal but at having had a miserable life. The guy didn't deserve someone as beautiful and caring as Liz for a daughter.

"She's fine, I'm sure."

"Really, can you be so sure?" Mac challenged with one eye brow lifted.

Jonathan waved a hand at Mac, dismissing his words. "Let's get back to the reason I'm here."

"You piece of shit, I thought you were cold for doing this to your own child, but you're so much more than cold, you're heartless."

"Elizabeth is resilient, she'll bounce back."

"Why you lousy sonofa—"

Liz stepped in front of him, planted a hand firmly on Mac's chest and warned him with her eyes. He hadn't even heard her step into the room.

"Don't." She pleaded with him.

Mac gritted his teeth. "Just one?" He wanted so badly to hit the guy.

Her lips curved up at the sides. "Maybe I'll let you deck him later." She turned to her father, who looked at her with utter shock. Her smile vanished, only hatred showed now. "After I'm done with him."

"What the hell is this?" Jonathan gave her robe a tug in repulsion.

She slapped his hand away, her lips curled up in disgust. "This is me cozying up to the man you hired to abduct me."

Cromwell wasn't an award winning actor for nothing; his face showed only what he wanted it to show. "I beg your pardon? I hired this man to work on one of my movies; he abducted you and has been blackmailing me for days."

Liz turned to Mac; her shocked expression would have

won her several awards. "Mackenzie, is this true? Have you been blackmailing my father?"

He pulled a cigarette from his pack and casually responded. "I'm not sure I would use as strong a word as blackmail."

"Threatening that you will reveal my involvement in this ordeal to the tabloids if I don't pay you two million dollars is what I call blackmail," Jonathan said in a snooty upper class tone.

"You just stuck your Gucci shoe right in your mouth, Daddy." She turned back to Mac. "Give us some time alone, okay?" When he hesitated, she touched his cheek softly to reassure him. "I'll be fine, really." She kissed him now, passionately, partially to piss her father off, mostly because Mac's protectiveness touched her deeply.

"Fine. I'll be right outside if you need me." He shot Jonathan a hate filled look as he left.

"Let's get you out of this trashy little place, Elizabeth." Grabbing hold of her arm, Jonathan tugged her towards the door.

She jerked it away and snarled. "Go to hell."

"Elizabeth!"

"Shut up and sit down." When he stared at her with contempt, she stiffened her back and spoke to him with absolute ice. "Don't tempt me to get the ropes Mac used to tie me up with, Daddy, the ones you told him to use on me."

"I had nothing to do with any of this."

Liz gave him a not so gentle shove that sent him tumbling into the chair behind him. The look he gave her might have stopped anyone else in their tracks, but Liz was through jumping at his commands. "I was here, right here," she pointed to the spot he sat in, "when you called yesterday, and I heard everything you said to Mac, so don't sit there with that hurt innocent look on your face because I know it's a load of crap."

She grabbed Mac's pack of cigarettes, her hand steady

as a rock as she lit one up. "I call the shots now, Daddy."

"Great, bravo for you Elizabeth, have you been sleeping with him the whole time?"

"That is none of your concern." The smoke floated before her, masking the snarled image on her face.

He crossed his legs, leaned back and wiped dust from his jacket. "So you're slumming again, I see."

Liz felt the heat build right from her toes until it nearly boiled over at her head. "You bastard."

"Elizabeth! I will remind you to watch your tongue when you speak to me."

"Oh, shut up." She whirled on her father. "Mac is a decent man, a good man, and I won't have you trashing him or his house."

He leaned forward, his dark green eyes filled with anger. "That man is the one that kidnapped you."

"At your orders, and all because you wanted fucking publicity,"

"Elizabeth, that is quite enough."

"It's Liz, it has always been Liz and if you'd taken just one moment to get to know me, you would have known I prefer Liz,"

"Fine, *Liz*," he emphasized her name with gritted teeth. "I do know you, I know you perfectly well. If you want to spit venom at me, my dear, I will tell you exactly why I did this." He narrowed his eyes. "I so hoped that this little ordeal would tame you, make you come to your senses, make you grow up, but instead I see you have once again decided to cozy up with trash."

The cigarette snapped in two. She set it in the ashtray, amazingly calm. "It brought me to my senses alright, and it showed me what a heartless bastard my father really is."

He stood, met his daughter's laser sharp eyes with his own. "I would watch how you speak to me, young lady."

With anger lacing her words, Liz stepped right in her father's face and spoke with absolute calmness. Inside she the anger bubbled. "And I would watch what you say to me, old man." She pulled the tiny tape recorder from her pocket; the very one she'd used to record her clearing Mac of any and all of his involvement. "I've been recording your every word."

His eyes moved from hers to the tape recorder she held in her hand. She could see the trickle of fear slide into his dark green eyes. "This is all I need, added to the tape Mac made yesterday, to prove everything. It should be enough to throw your sorry ass in jail for a good long time." She waved the recorder in his face. "Don't worry, Daddy, you've got your looks, you'll find a nice boyfriend to make the stay a little easier." She threw that in just for spite.

His hand came up so fast it shocked her when it connected with her cheek. He'd never hit her before. In a flash, she saw Mac charge into the room

"You son-of-a-bitch." Grabbing hold of the guy by his jacket front, Mac pushed him against the wall, pinning him. "You just made the biggest mistake of your life Cromwell." He lifted his free hand, fist ready.

"No, don't, Mac, he's not worth it." Her cheek stung, but there were no tears, only rage.

"Liz," Mac turned to her, still holding Cromwell up against the wall. "He deserves what he gets from me for that."

"He'll only use it against you, Mac. Please."

"You're fucking lucky, old man. I would count your lucky stars." He released him with a great deal of power.

Liz turned to her father, a strong and determined look on her face, hatred growing like a festering disease inside of her. "I'll see you rot in prison."

Jonathan turned from his angry daughter and snarled at Mac. "You put her up to this."

"No," Liz stepped in. "I put him up to it." She straightened her robe, took a deep breath. She was ready to make a stand for the first time in her life. "I found out you were behind this whole deal. I knocked Mac out, tied him up and forced him to go along with me."

A face well used to hiding his emotions suddenly burst with it. "That is just plain ridiculous. Look at him." He waved a hand at Mac.

"Shocking, I know, but she managed it," Mac supplied.

"Thanks to your insistence of me having a trainer, I'm quite strong," Liz boasted.

Gritting his teeth, Jonathan glared at his daughter. "Why?"

"Because I wanted revenge; I wanted you to pay for what you put me through, what you did, and what you thought more important than me, your career." She felt her body shaking and refused to acknowledge it.

"He played a part in it as well, yet you seem to have forgiven him?" Jonathan spouted dryly, his eyes cold as they shifted to Mac.

Liz leaned in real close to her father, her face took on a seriousness that wasn't often seen, and she laid her heart on the line. "Yes, you are absolutely right, I have forgiven him. And do you want to know why."

"I'm sure you're about to tell me, so get on with it already."

Liz stiffened her back, took a deep breath and let it flow. "I forgive Mac, because I'm in love with him."

Chapter 27

The room fell into complete silence with the revelation of what Liz had just said. No one spoke and Liz felt the tension swirling around her. She'd just opened herself up so completely, would she now have her heart ripped out?

"That's ridiculous." Jonathan finally stated.

Liz blinked, cocked her head to the side and replied, "'That's ridiculous', is that all you can say? I just told you I forgave Mac because I love him, and not you."

Jonathan pulled a thin imported cigar from the inside pocket of his suit jacket, slid it through his long manicured fingers. "Shall I hurt you by telling you the same thing? That I do not love you?"

She hadn't realized she could feel any more pain from him; she'd been mistaken. "You've made it painfully obvious how you felt for me over the years; this kidnapping scheme just confirmed it." She took a deep breath to calm herself. He made it clear how he truly felt, and Liz felt the cold distance slip between them. The time had come to end things once and for all.

"Okay, Mr. Cromwell, this is how it's going to happen. You will transfer ten million into Mac's bank account by closing today." She upped the stakes. Might as well make it a deep cut.

"Don't be ridiculous."

"Have it your way, then." Shrugging, Liz picked up the telephone and dialed. "I need a patrol car immediately for a domestic disturbance, yes, please hurry, the address is..." She turned to Mac, giving him a look that told him to just play along.

"281 Breckenridge Lane."

"281 Breckenridge Lane—" In a swift move, Jonathan yanked the phone from her grasp and disconnected it. Turning to her father, Liz smiled. "That will certainly help things along nicely, thank you."

"Call them back and explain differently," he

demanded, thrusting the telephone out to her, realizing his mistake.

"Oh, I'll explain everything when they get here." Liz looked at the man before her with absolute resolution, then calmly took a seat at the table. "How long do you think it will take them to get here, Mac?" She pulled out a cigarette and casually lit it up.

Mac ran a hand through his hair nervously. "Five minutes, ten tops."

"You have ten minutes to agree to our demands. If you don't, I will hand over all my evidence to the nice officers when they show up." She blew a stream of smoke at Jonathan, ignoring his scowl. She suddenly felt in control and proud of it.

"Then you'll be subjecting your lover to jail as well."

Mac thought the same thing. Was he going to be doing time after all, spending his life behind bars, fighting off the advances of big Bennie? Sweet God, what was he going to do?

"Mac won't do any time, he's innocent. He was threatened by you, blackmailed into it by you." Her voice steady. She would see to it that Mac was never held accountable for his actions, even if she needed to lie to do it.

"That is utterly ridiculous and completely untrue." Jonathan set his forgotten cigar in the ashtray.

"Is it? You must have been pretty damn desperate to get back in the limelight to convince the banks not to loan Mac the money he needed to save his home."

"I've had enough of this." Jonathan jumped to his feet; Liz pushed him down before he could try anything.

"Sit," she demanded with fiery eyes. He just confirmed what she'd thought. "As I see it, ten million is a small price to pay to keep this all out of the news." She drew on her cigarette slowly, giving them all time to settle down a bit. "Unless of course you want your career ruined and a long stint in jail?"

Kidnapped

Jonathan ran a nervous hand through his hair. He eyed his daughter and soon realized she meant every word.

"Five minutes and ticking, Mr. Cromwell." Liz tapped her wrist. It would have been better if she had actually been wearing a watch, but he got the point.

His eyes met hers and lit with fire. "You are a conniving little—"

"Watch it, Cromwell," Mac warned him with a protective hand on Liz's shoulder.

Narrowing his eyes, Jonathan turned back to Liz, fuming mad. "Fine, you win. I'll do it, and I will see to it that your inheritance is terminated as well as your belongings removed from my premises by closing today as well."

"You selfish bastard. How the hell can you—" Mac stopped when Liz put a hand up.

"I don't want your money and I don't need my belongings. You can burn them for all I care. I don't want anything to do with you ever again." She could sever the ties between them because they never really had any to begin with. Her father never held her when she'd been scared or when she'd been hurt. It wasn't her father who'd come to her school to discuss her work with the teachers, that had been the nanny. He hadn't cared for her as his child; his only care was for his precious image and that she do nothing to mar it. She was through being his puppet to play with when he chose and toss in a box when he was done. "We're through."

"Liz."

She silenced Mac's protest with her index finger; then drew on her cigarette. She meant every word.

Jonathan stared at the woman before him, actually admiring her guts. "Fine, but you'll come running back to me when you come to your senses." And he would make her pay for her deception.

She laughed now, flighty and filled with humor, her head tipped back. "I have come to my senses, old man, and

I wouldn't run to you if I was starving to death and living in a box under some bridge."

"We'll see." He picked up his cigar, relit it. "Now call off the cops."

"You call your accountant first." She handed him the phone. She knew him well enough to know how deceitful he could be.

Snarling, Jonathan grabbed it, dialed, then recited what needed to be done, explained he would be in later in the day to fill out the paperwork, then hung up. "Done, now you call off the police." He thrust the phone out at her.

Her lips curved up with utter wickedness. "I never called the police, I called for the time." *Gotcha, old man. Oh, lord, look at his face.* He was absolutely shocked and she loved it.

Jonathan's eyes widened in surprise. Standing, he straightened his jacket, stiffened his back and held his head high. "Clever little girl. You're willing to give up all you have, all the glamour, all the money, all the prestige, for this?" He lifted his hands to the room, then to Mac.

"In a heartbeat."

"So be it. Have your bank contact my accountant." He slipped a card from his pocket and handed it to Mac.

Mac took the card, laid it on the table, then did what he'd wanted to do for days. "Pleasure doing business with you." He saluted him one finger style, and got the perfect reaction. Jonathan sent him a contemptuous look.

"We'll see who's laughing in the end, Mr. Tyrell."

"No funny business, Mr. Cromwell, I still have the evidence." Liz held up the tape recorder, giving it a shake.

"I'll keep up my end of the bargain if you keep up yours," he warned her, then stepped from the house.

With one hardy shove, she slammed the door behind him. It closed with a loud snap, echoing in the silence. A definite sign of her severing ties with her father and meaning it. It was final now; she was officially on her own. God help her.

Kidnapped

Liz turned, slipping the tape recorder into the robe pocket and saw Mac sitting at the table, his eyes nearly glazed over. "Mac?"

"Give me a minute, okay?" Grabbing his cigarette package, he lit one up, taking a long slow drag.

"It's going to be okay."

His eyes lifted to hers, unsure. "How can you be so calm?"

She wasn't calm, by any means, but she needed to stay strong. "I don't know, maybe I'm just relieved."

"You severed all ties to your father, to your *father*, Liz."

"He may be my father genetically, but he's never been a father to me. Okay, yes, I realize what I did was drastic, maybe insane—"

"No maybes," Mac added, flicking ashes into the ashtray on the table. "Once you've both cooled down, you can talk it out and go back to the way things were."

"No," she said sternly, sitting down across from him. "I meant what I said, Mac, I never want to see him again."

"Liz, he's your father, family."

"Yes, family. Has your family ever hired someone to kidnap you? No. And why is that? Because they love you."

Love, there was that word again. "You need your father, Liz; you need his money."

It appalled her that he would think that. "You know, for years I went on taking his money because I felt he owed me something, if not love, then his money. Yes, I wasted my life, I should have gone to school, I should have done something more with my life, but I'm not dead and I am certainly not too old to change things. I don't need his money Mac, never did. All I ever wanted from him was his love."

"You said you loved me." His eyes lifted to hers. "Was that out of spite?"

"No." She could admit it now, what more did she have to lose.

"Liz," he sighed her name, tapping out his cigarette. "How can you love me when I've done so much to hurt you?"

She touched his hand softly, her eyes filling with emotions. "I don't understand it either, Mac, but I know what I feel. Yes, I hated you, at first, but deep down I felt something more. I was attracted to you even before I saw that gorgeous face of yours." She smiled now.

"I have nothing to offer you, Liz."

Her eyes widened in surprise. It was too much to expect him to feel anything for her. "You have plenty to offer me Mac, for starters, a job."

"A job?"

"Working on your ranch. I want to help, Mac, I really do. I don't know much about taking care of horses, but I want to learn. For the first time in my life, I want something more for myself, and when you mentioned what you wanted for your farm, I could actually see it, see myself here, working it with you." She lowered her head. "I don't expect you to love me back; I know that's too much to ask for."

He lifted her chin with his fingers, his eyes smiling into hers. "I want you, Liz; there is no question about that. But I have to know this isn't just a passing fancy." He couldn't open his heart to her just yet.

"I want this, Mac, I want you and I'm willing to do anything to prove to you that this, us, me loving you, is not just a passing fancy. Give me a chance, Mac, let me show you who I really am."

"Okay, princess, you have a deal." He held his hand out to her, waiting for her to take it.

She supposed she would have to do with that. Taking his hand in hers, she gasped when he yanked her over the table and shocked her with a sharp kiss.

"That should seal it." He smiled, brushing the hair from her face.

"I won't let you down, Mac, I promise."

Epilogue

It was a chilly winter, the kind that made you long for a warm sunny resort to bask in and enjoy a fruity drink. But those days were over for her now, and this was what she'd traded it for.

As Liz shoveled hay into the stalls, she sniffed in the aroma of horses, cold air and hay scented with urine and fecal matter. A year ago she might have turned her nose up at the scent, at the whole ordeal, but not now. Now she relished in it, thrived on it and loved every inch of the horse ranch she now called home. She had a home, finally a home, and it was the best thing that had ever happened to her.

"I think she's going to give us a beautiful foal."

Liz turned to Mac, her face red from the cold, her hair pulled up and under her wool cap, her face plain and smudged with dirt. She looked towards the horse Mac stroked and smiled. "Just like her mama." She stood, gave her back a rub and worked out the kinks.

"Stiff?"

"A little." She rested her arm on the rake in her hand and held the other out to the horse in the stall next to her. "I have to admit to you, though, the idea of giving birth scares the hell out of me."

"We'll have a vet here; he'll do most of the work."

"Easy for you to say, being a man. Isn't that right, honey?" Liz smiled, petting the horse's long brown mane. She'd learned a lot about horses since she and Mac had started the ranch. And if she foolishly once thought horses were easy to care for, she didn't think so now. She knew better. They took work, lots of back breaking hard work. But it was all worth it in the end.

Mac stepped to the side, hooking his arm over her shoulder. "You know if we could take over the burden, we men would."

Liz snorted; the horse seemed to understand and did

the same, bunting Mac in the side. "Right, and there wouldn't be enough sedatives in the world to calm you down. Men aren't equipped to deal with pregnancy, let alone giving birth."

"Well, in all fairness, we would have to have surgery to delivery the kid, and surgery is a lot harder to recover from than squirting a kid out of your privates, princess."

Liz rolled her eyes, set her rake aside to lean on the fence that separated them from the horses. "Oh yes, panting with each contraction that squeezes your insides until it feels like you're ready to pop, then giving you a moment's reprieve before another hits is a piece of cake. Not to mention the hours it takes to squeeze that kid out is as easy as this." She snapped her fingers then slugged his arm good and hard. "Moron."

"And you would know all about labour and delivery because...?"

She stretched her back, scratched her head. "Marissa and Olive explained it to me." Mac's two sisters-in-law, who she'd grown very attached to since first meeting them. With no sisters of her own, Marissa and Olive were the next best thing.

"I'm sure they did, and filled your head with horror stories. Besides, Olive had it easy. She popped all three out in less than three hours."

"And because it only took three hours, that makes it all better." She rolled her eyes. "Please."

"Fine, whatever. Just don't go getting chicken on me, princess. We agreed to do this together, no backing out now." He pulled the wool cap over her eyes and smiled.

Casually, she slipped the hat off her head, shook her long golden hair free. "Oh, I have no intentions of backing out of our agreement, Mac." She turned seductive eyes his way, smiling. "I couldn't now in any case."

"Oh and why is that?"

"Because I'm pregnant, dummy."

He heard the words but he stood there speechless. It

took the horse to nudge him in the butt for him to come to his senses. "For real?"

She laughed, and the sound echoed in the cool air. "No, I'm kidding." But the glee she saw on his face gave her hope.

"You're kidding?"

"Yes," she laughed.

"That's not nice." He wiped his brow, turning to the horse, his face screwed up in a frown.

"Awe, did I scare you, Mac?" She patted his cheek, snickering.

He turned to her, his face serious. "No, you didn't scare me."

"You seriously thought I was pregnant?"

"Yes, I did."

Was that disappointment she heard in is voice? "But we're not married."

"Why should that stop us?"

"It's just, well…" He hadn't even told her he loved her yet. And it had been months since professing her love to him.

He took her hand in his, pulled her closer. "Liz, don't you know how I feel about you yet? I love you."

Liz frowned. "Well, how am I supposed to know that when you've never told me?" She slapped his chest. "Jackass."

Laughing, he pulled her closer. "I had wanted to wait until New Year's Eve to do this, but hell, now is as good a time as any." From his pocket he pulled out a small black box. "Liz, will you marry me?"

"Oh, how romantic." She rolled her eyes when inside she giggled with glee.

"You're right, it isn't. I'll wait."

"No, stop." She took his hand before he could put the box back in his pocket. "I accept."

Laughing, Mac opened the box and held the ring out to her. "You haven't even seen the ring."

"I don't give a damn about the ring." She threw her arms around his neck and smothered him with hot mind numbing kisses. "Yes, yes, yes," she said with each kiss.

Laughing, Mac lifted her off her feet and spun her in a circle. "You amaze me, princess. With every day I see you out here working, getting filthy, I am continually amazed by you. You've come so far since we first met."

"Yeah, I have, haven't I? Now give me the ring."

Shaking his head, Mac pulled the ring from its case and held it out to her. "I went for a modest ring. Knowing your temper, I thought it was best—on my behalf, to go for small."

She caught the smirk in his eyes before she glanced down at the ring. Her eyes widened at the size of the rock. "Small, oh my god Mac, it's huge." Her eyes lifted to his, the tears of joy slid down her cheeks. "I really, really do love you."

He wiped the tears from her cheeks, then cupped her face in his hands. "And princess, I really, really love you too." He slipped the ring on her finger, then scooped her up in his arms and carried her to the house.

The End

About the Author:

Shiela Stewart has been writing for the better part of her 40 years, pouring her heart out in words, living a fantasy through the characters she creates. It has always been a dream of hers to have her work published, a dream she has finally seen come to life.

When not writing, she is busy working on two websites for organizations she belongs to, tending to her three children, and spending time with the love of her life, William.

Shiela has a deep affection for animals and it's evident in the four cats, one dog, eight fish and three turtles she owns. Aside from writing, she enjoys sketching, painting, singing and dancing, as well as stargazing, astronomy and astrology. Her favorite time of the day is sunset.

This is a publication of
Linden Bay Romance
WWW.LINDENBAYROMANCE.COM

Recommended Linden Bay Romance Read:

A Question of Sex by G.A. Hauser

Sharon Tice seems to have it all. She's beautiful, confident, sexy, and holds an executive position in her father's prestigious firm. But when her father puts her in charge of his latest building project, Sharon soon discovers that her life is missing something...Mark Antonious Richfield.

Mark is one of Los Angeles' most eligible bachelors, charming, charismatic and successful. His first encounter with Sharon takes him by complete surprise. The attraction between the two is undeniable and when they give in to the impulse to satisfy it, and one another, it's positively explosive.

After his first taste of Sharon, Mark is left wanting more, and the sultry blonde is more than willing until she's introduced to Jack, Mark's roommate, and begins to suspect that they are lovers. Somewhere between rumor and innuendo lies the truth. Will Sharon put aside her fears and jealousy long enough to discover the possibility of love? Or, will it simply remain A *Question of Sex*?

Made in the USA